On the Trail of John Brown's Body

Young Heroes of History

by
Alan N. Kay

WHITE MANE KIDS
SHIPPENSBURG, PENNSYLVANIA

This White Mane Books publication
was printed by
Beidel Printing House, Inc.
63 West Burd Street
Shippensburg, PA 17257-0152 USA

The acid-free paper used in this book meets the guidelines for permanence and durability of the Committee on Production Guidelines for Book Longevity of the Council on Library Resources.

For a complete list of available publications
please write
White Mane Books
Division of White Mane Publishing Company, Inc.
P.O. Box 152
Shippensburg, PA 17257-0152 USA

Library of Congress Cataloging-in-Publication Data

Kay, Alan N., 1965-
    On the trail of John Brown's body : young heroes of history / by Alan N. Kay.
        p. cm.
    Sequel to: Send 'em South
    Includes bibliographical references.
    Summary: Two young cousins and their fathers become involved in events leading up to abolitionist John Brown's raid on the federal armory at Harper's Ferry, West Virginia, in 1859.
    ISBN 1-57249-239-2 (alk. paper)
    1. Harpers Ferry (W. Va.)--History--John Brown's Raid, 1859--Juvenile fiction. [1. Harpers Ferry (W. Va.)--History--John Brown's Raid, 1859--Fiction. 2. Abolitionists--Fiction. 3. Fathers and sons--Fiction. 4. Cousins--Fiction.] I. Title.

PZ7.K178 On 2001
[Fic]--dc21
                                                                    2001026798

This book is dedicated to my good friend Regina Pratt: The best teacher I ever knew. She was the kind of hero this book is about.

Contents

Characters

George and David Adams—the main characters. They are cousins, who are young, teenage Irish boys living in Boston.

Sean Adams—George's father

Jonathan Adams—David's father

Regina Adams—David's mother

William—David's grandfather, Regina's father

Mary, Helen, and Thomas—David's younger sisters and brother

Uncle Robert—father of Joshua, Zachary, Ethan, Rachel, and Jamie, cousins who live in the bottom apartment

Aunt Patricia—Uncle Robert's wife

Charles Bishop—a boy from Kansas

Abe Bishop—Charles' father

Preface

Young Heroes of History focuses on children and young adults who were heroes in their time. Although they may not have achieved fame or fortune, they made a difference in the lives of those near to them. Many were strong in body and spirit, but others managed to do the best they could in the time and place in which they lived.

Although the heroes of this series are fictional, these young Americans are placed in situations that were very real. The events of the time period as well as many of the people in these stories are accurately based on the historical records. Sometimes the language and actions of the people may be hard to understand or may seem inappropriate, but this was a different time.

Introduction

George and David Adams were not only cousins, they were best friends. They played baseball together, chased each other through the streets of Boston together, went to school together, and even got into trouble together. Most of the time the trouble that they caused was just harmless kid pranks: making fun of the teacher in school, skipping classes, or staying up all night in the city. But as the boys grew older and the problems in the country worsened, the trouble began to get serious.

Northerners and Southerners were arguing constantly about slavery. Men like John Brown and others had begun to murder people. Laws had been passed to protect the slave owners but not the slaves. David's parents who were abolitionists (people who wanted to free the slaves) hated these laws. Already his parents had broken the law several times by hiding escaped slaves. David and George tried to not worry about all these problems as they played like normal boys.

But sooner than they expected, the trouble found them. Having stumbled upon a young slave girl named Lisa hiding in Boston, David and George decided to help her escape from the slave catchers. Unfortunately, after quite an adventure in which they ran throughout the city and David almost got killed, they were unable to save her.[1] Standing on the dock in Boston Harbor, watching Lisa be returned to slavery, David swore that he would do something else to help his slave friend, and George, as usual, went along for the ride. What neither boy knew was that this small adventure would eventually lead them on a trail of danger and violence that could either make them heroes or destroy not only their family but the entire country.

---

1. You can read all about this adventure in book one, *Send 'Em South*, of the Young Heroes in History Series.

Chapter 1
Burglars

"I knew this was a bad idea," George mumbled as he lifted another small statue off his grandfather's mantle and looked underneath it.

"I didn't hear you complaining when we discussed it back home," replied George's cousin David, who was across the darkened room looking through a chest of drawers.

"That's cuz you said it would be easy," George quickly replied.

"It will be easy," David answered. "All we gotta do is look around until we find the money and then we take off."

"But what if he comes home?" George asked as he moved toward a cabinet and began looking through his grandfather's papers.

"He ain't gonna come home," David said directly. "I told you already that when I met with him earlier today to ask for help he kept looking nervously at the clock and trying to get me to leave. He repeated over and over again that he had someplace important to be tonight."

"Yeah, well fine," George agreed with a wave of his hand to cut David off. "But what if there ain't any money here?"

"There's gotta be," David said firmly yet anxiously. "Grandpa always talks about saving money for a rainy day and he's always looking around the room suspiciously whenever we ask him about his money."

"Yeah, like he's got a secret that he don't want anyone to find out," George added with a grin. "But where do you think it is?"

"I'm not sure," David answered. "But it's gotta be in this room somewhere. It's where he keeps all of his important stuff. You try over there; I'm gonna look in his desk."

David began rifling through the drawers in his grandfather's desk while George looked for a hidden panel or a wall safe behind one of the hanging pictures. Despite their bold words, both boys were extremely afraid that their grandfather would return and catch them. He was not a nice man, at least not to them, and he would certainly be furious with them if they were caught. He might send them to the police, George thought.

The boys had never liked their grandfather, even though he had been the one who had helped the family get out of the Irish slums of Boston. He rented them an apartment and then helped David's father, Jonathan, and George's father, Sean, find jobs at the plant where he worked. Unfortunately, he only did it because his daughter had married David's father. He disliked them all, constantly reminding them that he did not like the Irish and that he was against his daughter's marriage from the start. It was only because he loved his daughter so and because she did not become a Catholic when she married that he allowed the relationship. Furthermore, he would always make fun of their traditions and treat his grandchildren like they were pets instead of people. It made George angry every time he thought of it. Now, with his "dirty Irish hands" all over his grandfather's precious collections he smiled as he imagined the look on his grandfather's face when he found his money missing.

"What did Grandpa say when you asked him for help?" George asked, breaking the sudden silence.

"He said he couldn't use his money to save some slave all the way down in Savannah because he needed it to fight slavery in other 'grander' ways," David answered. "And he couldn't help repeating again and again that if I hadn't messed things up in the first place, then maybe Lisa would be on her way to Canada now instead of being returned to slavery."

"That wasn't your fault," George responded in anger. "You did everything you could to help her, it wasn't your fault that—"

"Whatever, whatever, George," David interrupted with a wave of his hand. "I don't wanna talk about this. Let's just find the money so we can get out of here."

"Okay, okay," George agreed, turning his back to David while he examined the wall some more. Ever since he and David had found Lisa, the escaped slave, and tried to help her, David had become a different person. He had done strange things like skipping school, hiding in the slums, and now getting George to steal from his grandfather. George wondered whether it was all worth it. "After all," he thought, "she was only colored."

"Hey, what's this?" David said suddenly, holding up a plain, white envelope.

"Did you find something?" George asked as he rushed toward David.

"I dunno," David replied, holding the envelope up to the window so he could see it clearer in the moonlight. "It feels like it might have money in it and it says something on the front."

"What's it say?" George asked.

"I'm not sure," David replied squinting. "I think it says...Brown."

"Brown?"

"Yeah, it says Brown," David answered.

"What's that supposed to mean?" George asked.

"I don't know," David said shrugging his shoulders. "But who cares? Let's see what's inside."

David slowly opened the envelope and reaching inside it, he pulled out a piece of paper wrapped around several dollar bills hidden inside.

"Wow!" George whispered slowly. "How much is in there?"

"It looks like it could be as much as fifty dollars!" David cried.

"Fifty dollars!" George exclaimed. "Why that's enough to buy your own horse."

"Maybe two horses," David said gleefully.

"What's the paper say?" George reminded him.

"I'm not sure," David answered, stuffing the money into his pocket and squinting at the small writing. "It's a bunch of names and dollar amounts."

"What's it for?" George asked.

"I don't know," David replied as he stuffed the paper into his other pocket. "But let's not worry about that now. We better..."

"Yes, I know what you mean, Steven," a voice from the other room suddenly said as they heard the outside door opening.

"Oh my God!" George whispered.

"Grandpa's here!" David exclaimed. "Quick, hide!"

David jumped behind the couch against the wall while George ran into a closet near the desk. Just as he was closing the closet door, George saw his grandfather walk into the room with another man.

"But are you sure we can trust him?" George could hear the other man say.

"Do we have any choice?" George's grandfather replied.

"No, I suppose not," the other man answered. "There certainly is no one else who is willing to go to such measures."

"When did you first hear of it, Steven?" Grandfather asked as he sat on the couch that David was hiding behind. David crouched nervously trying to breathe as softly as possible. His heart raced and he began to sweat. It was as though the two men were sitting right on top of him.

"Back in the spring, Minister Parker first mentioned it to me in private after one of his sermons."

"Yes, me too," Grandfather added, "but in my case, it was I who approached the minister."

"You approached him?" Steven seemed surprised.

"Why yes, I had been saving my money for several months, looking for some way I could help but not really sure what to do."

"What were they talking about?" David wondered. "Was Grandpa involved in something with his minister?"

"I thought you sent your money to your daughter in Kansas."

"Mom," David thought suddenly. "They're talking about my mother."

"No, no. She insisted on doing everything on her own. All I did was give money to the Emigrant Aid Society."

"Yes, but the society then helped her."

"When were they going to leave?" George thought. He was getting scared inside the closet without an idea of what he could do.

"Yes, the society did help her," Grandfather answered. "They helped anyone from New England trying to settle in Kansas. But, since Regina had to do everything on her own, she did not feel like I was giving her a handout."

"Good old mom," David thought, "proud as ever."

"How long has she been gone?" Steven asked.

"Oh, just over two full years now," Grandfather answered.

"Do you hear from her often?"

"I used to, but recently she has been late in corresponding to me. I am beginning to wonder if something is wrong."

"Oh no," George pleaded to himself. "Don't start talking about Kansas and Aunt Regina."

"Do you suspect foul play?" Steven asked.

"No, not really, but look," he said, slapping Steven on the knee and standing up, "you didn't come here to talk about my daughter, you came to discuss our fundraising."

"Whew," George thought to himself when his grandfather changed the subject. George knew that if his grandfather started talking about Kansas and his daughter they could be there for hours.

"How much have you managed to collect?" Steven asked as he followed George's grandfather.

"Well, I've already sent several hundred ahead, but I have almost fifty dollars in the desk here now," Grandpa said proudly as he made his way to the desk.

"Oh, no!" David thought suddenly. "He's headed toward the desk. He's gonna find that the money is missing. What do I do?"

David looked around. He couldn't run to the door. They would easily see him. He looked up. There was a window directly above him behind the couch. If he could slowly raise his hand up to open the window while their backs were turned, he might be able to slip out unnoticed.

George was panicking. They were coming towards the desk next to the closet where he was hiding, and they would discover the missing money. If he tried to run he would bang right into them.

"What was David doing?" he thought desperately.

David had his hand on the window now. He pushed up gently. It was open!

"I've been keeping it in this bottom desk drawer," Grandfather said to Steven as he sat down in the chair. "I know that it is the only place that my wife won't touch."

"I know what you mean," Steven said with a chuckle. "I can't keep anything from my wife either."

David had the window all the way open now.

"Hey, where is it?" Grandfather said loudly. "It was right under these papers in this drawer."

"Are you sure?" Steven asked.

"Of course I'm sure," Grandfather answered angrily. "I keep it right here under my paperweights."

"Wait," Grandfather interrupted himself. "My paperweights have moved...and this drawer is open...someone's been in here."

David knew it was now or never. He looked up, saw that the two men were looking the other way, and jumped out the window.

"Sorry, George," David whispered as he landed on the sidewalk and began to run.

"Look, the window is open!" Steven said suddenly.

"Someone has been here!" Grandfather shouted. "And they've stolen my money!"

Chapter 2
Caught

Bang, bang, bang! a fist pounded on the door.

George's father, Sean, shrugged in his sleep.

Bang, bang, bang! the fist slammed again.

"Open up in there!" a voice yelled from the outside.

"Ugghhh," Sean groaned as he rolled out of bed and stood up shakily. "Just a minute!"

Sean reached to the floor to find his shirt and pants. The heat of the summer sun cooked the upstairs apartment like an oven, so Sean slept in as little clothing as possible.

Bang, bang, bang! again on the door. "Open up, Sean, it's William!"

"What is it, Uncle Sean?" George's older cousin Mary asked sleepily from her bed across the room. She, David, and their younger brother and sister shared the upstairs apartment with George and his father.

"Nothing, Mary," Sean answered as he slipped his other leg into his pants. "It's just your grandfather at the door, go back to sleep."

Bang, bang...

Sean flung the door open.

"What's going on, William?" Sean said angrily. "Why are you waking me up this late at night with—"

"George?" his father, Sean, shouted in surprise. "What are you doing out there?"

"The young hooligan was stealing money from me," William answered as he flung George at his father. "And now he won't tell me where it is!"

"You what?" George's father yelled in shock.

"I...I...I'm sorry, Dad," George stuttered as he landed hard against his father's chest. "David made me do it. I really didn't want to!"

"What is going on?" Sean growled at Grandfather.

"All I know," Grandfather replied, "is that I found your son hiding in my closet and that fifty dollars was stolen from my desk tonight."

"David!" Sean yelled as he turned back into the apartment. "David Adams! Get over here!"

No response. The other children began to stir in their beds.

"David!" Grandfather yelled as well.

Sean found his lantern and lit it. The room was suddenly bathed in an eerie yellow light, yet David was nowhere to be seen.

"He's not here," Sean said holding the lantern over David's unslept bed. "It looks as though he hasn't been here all night."

"He ran off," George said quickly, trying to keep the attention on David instead of him. "He's taken all the money and he ain't coming back."

"What money?" Sean asked.

"My money, you idiot," Grandfather answered shortly turning to George. "Where has he run off to, boy, and why did you steal my money in the first place?"

"It was David's idea," George repeated. "I really didn't want to do it."

"You've already said that," George's father said in a huff. "Now tell us what this is all about or you'll get punishment like you've never seen before."

"Well, it's all about that colored slave girl," George began.

"You mean the fugitive slave you boys brought to me last month?" George's father asked.

"Yeah," George answered. "Well anyway, you know that David's been acting crazy ever since, hiding her in our house, hanging out with the abolitionists, hiding in the slums and running around at night—"

"I know all about this, now get to the point," his father interrupted.

"Ummmmm, well after Lisa was caught and sent back to Georgia, David was acting even more crazy, especially after Uncle Robert whipped him. He started talking about saving her and finding his mom and dad and getting them to—"

"Is that what this is all about?" Grandfather said with a sudden realization. "David came to me today whining, complaining, and begging me to give him money to help his poor slave girlfriend."

"Yeah," George answered. "After he left your house he came to tell me that he wanted to steal your money."

"And you just went along with that?" George's father said in shock.

"Well, I...uh, no I didn't *just* go along with him," George answered nervously. "I told him that it was a stupid idea and that we'd get caught."

"But you still went along with him."

"Uhhhhhhh," George had no idea what to say.

"Well, this is just wonderful," Grandfather suddenly spoke up. "Here I am in the middle of the night with a young Irish boy who doesn't know right from wrong, my money has been stolen, and my eldest grandson has run off on some wild adventure to save some slave girl."

"Uhhhh, Grandpa, I don't think he just ran off," George said awkwardly. "I think he went to find his mom and dad."

"You do?" Grandfather asked. "And why do you think that?"

"Cuz ever since Lisa was caught," George continued, "David's been saying how his daddy would know what to do and that his daddy could've saved her."

"That does make some sense, William," Sean added. "Fifty dollars ain't nearly enough for him to do anything on his own to save that slave, but it's plenty to get him to Kansas."

"Well then, you'll have to get him for me, won't you?" Grandpa suddenly said to Sean.

"What?" both Sean and George cried.

"Of course you must," Grandfather persisted. "If it weren't for you, David would have never run off in the first place. Besides, I need someone to check on my daughter anyway. I haven't heard from her in quite awhile and I am beginning to worry. You'll leave as soon as you are able."

"Now just hold on a minute, old man," Sean interrupted. "You can't tell me what to do."

"Can't I?" Grandfather replied with a smug look on his face. "I got you that job remember. And even though you've done a good job keeping it, I could still talk to a few friends to make sure you lose it."

"You wouldn't," Sean said slowly.

"I certainly would," Grandfather responded. "I have had enough of this family. I tolerate you because of my daughter, but she is gone now and I am getting sick of renting this apartment to you and your brother anyway. I could easily rent it to someone else, someone who didn't cause as much trouble as your son here."

George glared at his grandfather.

"In fact," Grandfather continued, "let's up the stakes. I'll forget about getting the money if you and your son go to Kansas and ensure that my daughter is alright. Let her keep whatever money David has left. If you succeed then we never need to talk of these matters again. But, if you fail, I will see to it that your jobs are destroyed; I will evict you from this apartment; and you, your brother, and your family will be thrown out on the street just like all the other good-for-nothing Irish here in Boston."

"You're crazy," Sean responded.

"Perhaps," Grandfather answered, "but if I am, it is you and your family who have made me so. Do we have a deal?"

"It seems as if we have no choice," Sean answered.

"No you don't," Grandfather said as he turned towards the exit.

"Oh, and one more thing," he said abruptly as he turned around and glared at the family. "There was a piece of paper in the envelope with the money that I must have returned. It contained all kinds of information for my record books. If you fail to get that as well you will be evicted!"

Grandfather then turned again, walked out of the apartment, and slammed the door behind him.

Chapter 3
Good-byes

I t took almost a month for George and his father to get ready for the trip. They had asked around at the train station and found enough people who could confirm that David had indeed taken the train to New York. From there he would switch trains again and again, eventually getting close enough to Kansas to take a short stagecoach to the town of Lawrence where his parents lived. Unfortunately, Sean only had a little money saved, so George had to quit school to get a job. His father, Sean, had to borrow some money from his friends and from his brother Robert.

"It's bad enough I have to give you this money," George's Uncle Robert said to Sean as he handed him some cash. Of course he had waited until the last minute to give it to Sean, because he didn't believe they would go. But now that they were standing outside the house with their horses saddled, it was clear that they were ready to leave. "But to think that my whole family may be kicked out of the house because of you and that brat David—"

"Oh shut up, Robert," Sean interrupted quickly. "I'm sick of you blaming David and his parents for all your problems. If you hadn't beaten David so badly that night maybe he would have never run off."

"The brat was hiding a colored person!" Robert yelled back.

"Yeah, he was," Sean answered. "But that ain't what bothered you. You were upset because you weren't in charge."

"That's ridiculous," Robert said doubtfully.

"Is it?" Sean asked. "Ever since we moved into this house you've been so caught up with being the boss that it don't matter what anyone does as long as you get your way."

"You're darn right I have to get my way," Robert agreed. "I'm the oldest brother in this family and with mom and dad both dead that leaves me in charge."

"Oh, Robert," his wife, Patricia, interrupted. "Let's not start this again. I am so tired of you reminding us that you are the oldest brother. We all know that and I'm sure Sean means no harm in what he's saying, do ya Sean?"

"Well, no," Sean answered slowly. He didn't really agree with his sister-in-law, but at least she was getting Robert to shut up.

"See?" Patricia asked Robert. "He's not threatening you, Robert. Now let's just forget about this and say good-bye. Sean and George have a ways to go today and we can't be delaying them anymore."

"Fine, fine," Uncle Robert gave in. He never could win a fight with his wife anyway.

"Good luck, Sean," he said, walking towards his brother and shaking his hand. "Take care of yourself and say hello to John and Regina for us."

"I will, Robert," Sean answered. "And you take good care of yourself and all the kids too."

George looked around at his cousins. All nine of them had lined up to say good-bye. In one group there were his Uncle John's children, and in another there were his Uncle Robert's. He loved all of them in different ways, but his favorite was Thomas. He was only one year younger than George and had been more of a playmate than a cousin. Almost every day after school the three of them, Thomas, David, and George, would run around Boston looking for some place to hang out or some mischief to get into. Now, with David already run off and George on his way, Thomas would be all alone.

"Hey, cheer up, Thomas," George said lightly. "David and I will be back real soon and by then you'll be able to throw David some real fast balls."

"Really?" Thomas said with his eyes lighting up. The boys had only recently begun to play baseball, but already David had earned the reputation of being the home run king. Thomas would cheer for his older brother all the time and dream of hitting the ball as hard as he did.

"Sure and I'll bet you'll even strike him out once in awhile," George said with a grin.

"Yeah, well, just make sure you bring him back so I can beat him up some more," George's cousin Joshua interrupted. "I still owe him for the last match."

Standing next to Uncle Robert were his sons Joshua, Zachary, and Ethan along with his wife, Patricia, and their daughters, Rachel and Jamie. George did not get along as well with them. They lived downstairs and didn't go to school like he and David did. Still, they were fun to play with and George would certainly miss the long dinners with them as they listened to Aunt Patricia's stories or watched David and Joshua wrestle on the floor.

"Don't worry, I'll bring him back," George answered as he mounted his horse and readied himself for the ride. He took one last look at Thomas and smiled when he saw little Helen, who was still like a baby even though she was already five. George laughed a little as he watched Helen stroking her doll's hair and wondered whether she truly understood what was happening.

"You'd better," Mary said. She was the oldest girl in the family and she was already looking more like a woman than a girl. "It won't be any fun bossing people around if you and David aren't here to complain."

George smiled as he turned to his dad.

"Ready, George?" his father asked as he too mounted his horse. They had been able to buy two horses for the long ride to Kansas since they felt that would be the easiest way to follow David. It had been difficult finding a horse that was small enough for George yet strong enough to make the trip. They could have taken the stagecoach or several different trains along the new railroad lines, but they wanted their free-dom when they got to the open Kansas prairie.

"Ready, Dad," George answered nervously.

"Good-bye, everyone," George's father yelled.

"Good-bye!" they all shouted, waving their arms in the air.

"Be careful and come back soon!" George heard his Aunt Patricia call.

"Yah!" George's father yelled as he gently kicked his horse with his feet.

"Yah!" George repeated.

As they headed away, George looked back at his family waving. They were all in a big semicircle huddled close together. Thomas and little Helen were holding their big sister Mary's hand. George nervously held his horse's reins with one hand as he waved back as well. He listened to the slow clip-clop of the horses' hooves on the cobblestone streets. His family was still waving to them. Finally, as he rounded the corner, he turned one last time and saw them lower their hands and head into the house.

"Good-bye," George whispered one last time as he turned forward and looked at the road ahead.

A figure stepped out of the shadows once the fam-ily had disappeared.

"Did you get a good look at him?" Grandfather asked the man.

"Sure did." The man was dressed in a long, black trenchcoat that was open enough to allow a person to see the gun-belt underneath. He wore a gray hat on top of his jet black hair, and he had a fluffy mustache that almost hid his entire upper lip.

"Now don't forget," Grandfather continued, "you are not to be seen unless—"

"Unless I'm sure the kid has the paper," the man finished for Grandfather. "I know, I know. You told me a hundred times to follow the kid, find his cousin David, and find out who has the paper. Then, I'm to get the paper and return it to you or destroy it."

"Yes, that's right," Grandfather nodded. "But remember, no one is to be hurt, especially my daughter, Regina."

"What if the kid has memorized all the information on the paper?" the man asked with a slight grin.

"Uh...well," Grandfather mumbled nervously.

"Do you want people to find out about your involvement?" the man asked quickly.

"No, of course not," Grandfather answered quickly. "It's just that—"

"You don't want to kill your grandson?" the man finished again.

"Well, of course not," Grandfather said slowly.

"You keep telling me it's for a greater cause," the man reminded him.

Grandfather's face showed anger as he stood up straight and stared at the man.

"You don't need to remind me about the cause," he scolded. "Just do your job."

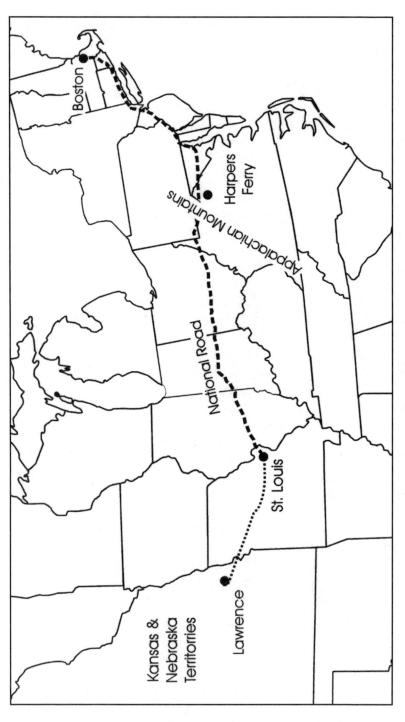

George and Sean's route to Kansas

Map by Alan N. Kay

Chapter 4
The Road

I t was the most exciting thing George had ever seen: Huge Conestoga wagons, led by six large horses of various shapes and colors, with their white tops puffing up like sails in a wind and their large wooden wheels slicing through the rock roared by on their way to deliver goods from one city to another. Anxious farmers marched their herds of confused and frightened cows or pigs down the road. Adventurous settlers brought their entire families with everything they owned on wagons or horses or mules. Speedy stagecoaches raced along carrying travelers from one city to another. Individual riders like George and his father rode by waving hello, or sometimes a mail carrier would rush past them in a flash. Bells would tingle, or people would yell at the top of their lungs as they rushed through the overcrowding on their way to wherever they were going.

George and his father had been traveling on this road for several weeks now and not a day had gone by without George seeing something new. Their route had taken them from Boston through New York, Philadelphia, and Baltimore offering them many new and exciting things to see; however it still didn't compare to the sights on the National Road.

This particular road had been started almost 50 years ago. Starting in Cumberland, Maryland, it was the main highway to the new western settlements as well as a major highway for travelers and traders alike. When gold was discovered in California 10 years ago the road was flooded with so many travelers that occasionally people could be delayed for days waiting for traffic to clear. It was an incredible piece of construction, George had thought as he crossed over the many bridges and rode along the crushed stone surface. The road noise was infinitely better than the dust that was kicked up or the countless potholes appearing in the unfinished sections of the road.

The best thing about this trip was that George and his dad were finally together. Ever since he was little, George could remember his father working late hours, seven days a week at the plant. Then, after his mother died, it only worsened. George never saw his dad except for meals and family holidays. Perhaps that was why David and George were so close. Neither of them had their father around, and David, who was a little older than George, sort of acted like a big brother.

Now with David and the rest of the family out of the picture, George had his father all to himself. They rode alongside one another the entire time, except when George would get the sudden urge to race and would whip his horse's reins to jump ahead of his father. George figured that his dad was letting him win because George definitely had a smaller horse. But it still was fun to beat him. In the evening, as the traffic died down, they would have long conversations about the family living in Boston and Ireland. George loved to hear his father tell of life back in the old country. He was not as good a storyteller as his Aunt Patricia, but

George discovered that he loved hearing about the simple life of his father at home on the farm with aunts, uncles, and cousins—more relatives than George could believe—all laughing, crying, fighting, and working together. Life there was so different from America that George occasionally wondered whether the stories were all true.

"Dad, did all those people really die in the famine?" George asked one day while they were riding on their way through Maryland.

"Of course they did," George's father answered a little angrily. The famine was always a delicate topic because so many Irish had lost their lives. George knew that he would have to be careful with what he said.

"But whole families?" George questioned softly. "Entire villages? How could a bad potato crop cause so many deaths?"

"The potato was everything to us," his father answered. "We were all farmers, George, you know that. No big cities, no factories, just simple folk trying to live everyday as it came to us."

"I know," George answered. "It sounds neat."

"Neat?" his father repeated.

"Yeah," George explained. "No noise, no school, no working in sweaty factories, nobody making fun of you and calling you Irish dirt. Just one big happy family."

"That's true," his father answered. "But we weren't always happy. There were lots of bad times and lots of fights. When the potato crop went bad everyone turned against each other and fought over whatever food remained. Families broke apart and wandered the streets begging for food. Children stole from their parents. I even heard stories of some mothers and fathers hiding food from their kids because there wasn't enough to go around."

"That's why you came to America?" George added even though he knew the answer.

"Yup," his father replied. "After your grandma died, your Uncle Robert, Uncle John, and I headed to America like everyone else."

"But what about mom?" George asked. "Was she here already or did her family come to America as well?"

"They came about the same time," George's father answered slowly. His face became soft and his brow wrinkled as he thought sadly of George's dead mother. "Even settled in the same part of Boston as we did."

"Fort Hill?" George asked.

"Yeah," his father answered. "But look, George. You know most of this already and it's getting late. Let's look for a place to stay."

George bowed his head in disappointment. He was looking forward to hearing more about his mother. His father never talked about her and George was hoping now that they were alone he would finally get the chance.

"There's a place up ahead," George's father said, pointing down the road at a small wooden house. "Let's check it out."

The inn was very much like all the others. There were several rooms with beds, a kitchen that served meals to the weary travelers, and a bar for those who felt the need to drink. Every night they stayed in a different inn. George got to stay up as late as he wanted, he got to eat whatever he wanted, and he even tried a beer once in awhile when his father was feeling really relaxed. His dad was really neat, George thought over and over again.

Of course the traveling was not always fun. They were never sure how far they would make it each day, so they had to hope there would be lodging whenever they stopped. Fortunately for them, this road was so well traveled that there was always a place to stay. Some of the inns were nice and comfortable with a restaurant downstairs that served a hearty breakfast. Other times they chose an inn which was merely a man's farm that he had converted into a roadhouse by adding a room here or there and taking advantage of all the travelers along the road. Once in awhile, George and his father had to take turns sleeping for fear that some lowlife would try to steal their belongings. Occasionally, George had the eerie feeling that they were being followed but he figured it was his imagination.

"Dad, you see that guy?" George said one morning at an inn in Indiana.

"What guy?" his father asked impatiently as the waiter approached.

"More coffee, sir?" he asked.

George's father nodded slowly as his head dropped like a deadweight. The waiter filled the cup to the brim for the third time. George wondered whether they would ever leave. They had gotten another late start this morning after George's father slept through the sunrise. He claimed that he had a headache, but George knew he was hung over from all the beer that he drank the night before.

"The guy in the black trenchcoat sitting in the corner," George whispered.

"What about him?" his father said, turning his head slowly.

"I could swear I've seen him before," George whispered again.

"He does look familiar," George's father agreed as he sipped more coffee.

"I think he's been following us," George declared.

"Don't be ridiculous," his father said. "Even if we have seen him before, he may just be headed in the same direction we are. I've seen lots of people over and over again."

"But why is he here so late in the morning?" George suggested.

"Maybe he has a headache too," his father groaned.

"But, Dad, I think maybe—"

"Look, George," his father interrupted, holding his forehead with one hand and raising the other in a stopping motion. "I'm not up for this. Just stop with your overactive imagination, and go upstairs and pack our bags. O.K.?"

"O.K., Dad," George agreed slowly. He looked again at the corner table and noticed the man was gone. "I guess I have been overreacting."

George headed upstairs to his room, leaving his father alone to finish his coffee.

"Overactive imagination," George repeated to himself. "I guess I do have one. The guy probably is on his way to Kansas or St. Louis too and we keep bumping into each other. I'll probably see him again before..."

George stopped. The door to their room was opened slightly.

"I know we locked it," George thought quickly. "There must be someone in there."

George walked up the stairs slowly, trying to peer into the room as he got closer. He thought about getting his father but he knew his dad would make fun of him saying he was imagining things again.

Reaching the room, he slowly poked his head inside. Across the room with his back towards him, George saw a man, wearing dark brown boots and a black trenchcoat, looking through their belongings.

"Hey, what are you doing?" George called out suddenly.

The man spun around in surprise, whipped out a gun, and pointed it at George. The man's jet black hair flew out from under his hat, and he wore a thick mustache that almost completely covered his upper lip.

George stepped back in fear putting his hands high in the air.

"Hey, don't shoot," George called out quickly. "I'm just a kid. I can't hurt you. I ain't even got a gun."

The man looked back and forth at the door and at the window. Then, without a word, he ran to the window, opened it, and jumped landing on a pile of hay below. George ran to the window to see where he had gone—the man had disappeared.

Chapter 5
The Prairie

George and his father quickly searched the area but could not find the man anywhere. Then they thoroughly checked their bags and still could find nothing missing. "What kind of a thief doesn't steal anything?" they wondered. So with nothing to report and nothing lost, and deciding the guy was just strange, they continued on their journey. This time, however, they were a little more careful. George, a little more nervous, never left his dad alone and he always locked the door of their room.

Eventually the road ended in Vandalia, Illinois. They were able, however, to keep traveling easily enough on a different road to St. Louis. Once in Missouri it was a little trickier getting across the state. After they left Kansas City and entered into the Kansas Territory (often called K.T. by the locals) things really began to change.

Once they left the outskirts of the small towns (there were no big towns and certainly not any cities, at least not like they had back East) they generally traveled the open prairie. It was an incredible sight and in some ways it reminded George's father of Ireland. It was more like a living thing than land. The tall, bright green grasses waved in the wind like waves approaching a shore. Wildflowers danced in the breeze flinging their petals into the air like rice being tossed at a bride and groom. Nature gave the air a sweet, refreshing scent that was so different from the smells of Boston, even when the sea breeze blew in off the harbor. George couldn't help but take deep, deep breaths as he held the crisp air in his lungs for as long as he could. It seemed as though the whole prairie was his. For as far as he could see there was nothing and no one else around him. The few hills and trees that blocked his vision were few and far between, so for the most part it seemed as though you could see prairie all the way to the horizon.

Birds sang in the air and swooped down to catch rodents and other animals with their claws. Sometimes entire flocks of them would fly by in such large numbers that the sky looked to be filled with huge black clouds. There were all kinds of animals which George had never seen. Foxes, deer, skunks, jackrabbits, and badgers roamed the prairie, casually sniffing around or at times bolting away from some unseen danger. Life seemed to be everywhere, even in the air buzzing around him.

The insects were not annoying during the day. For the most part the flies swarmed around George's horse instead of him, and as long as they moved at a relatively fast pace, the wind kept most of the bugs away. At night the insects were at their worst. Huge fireflies flew around George. It seemed as though millions of tiny lanterns were being carried in the air. George would run around and catch one in his hand, hold it gently, and wait for the little creature to light again. Then, he would laugh and throw it back into the air. The worst problem, of course, was the mosquitos. They swarmed everywhere, even a well-lit fire did not seem to repel them. Fortunately, George's father had been smart enough to stop in Kansas City to get some important supplies including some animal grease that he had been told the Indians used to keep the little buggers away. As long as you put the grease on your skin around dusk and reapplied it once in awhile, you could usually make it through the night with only a few bites.

This whole world of nighttime on the prairie proved to be a new experience for George. The stars shone so brightly, and the sky appeared clear and cloudless for miles and miles, making the whole universe seem open to him. Everywhere that George looked there was some kind of light to behold. In some places a few stars twinkled on their own; in other spots the countless number of stars appeared to form huge clouds of white. It was unlike anything he had seen in the city. There were so many shooting stars streaking across the sky on a regular basis that George began to run out of wishes. It was at times like this, sitting under the nighttime sky and listening to the fire sizzle, the insects buzz, and the crickets and frogs converse, that George felt the closest to his dad. They were all alone in this beautiful land and they could talk about anything.

"Dad, do you ever think of Mom?" George suddenly said, breaking the silence one night under the stars.

"Sure I do," his father replied. "Every night in fact."

"Really?" George asked.

"Sure," he said. "She was the most important person in my life, other than you of course. She was a special lady, always thinking about others before herself."

"Aunt Patricia makes her sound like a saint," George said.

"Well, she just might have been," his father answered. "She never worried about herself. She was always asking others how they were doing. She never rested until I was well fed and taken care of. Then when you were born it seemed like she never slept at all."

"I don't even remember her," George said sadly.

"I know, son," his dad said slowly, patting George on the head. "You were still an infant when she died, but believe me, she loved you more than any person could love another. I swear."

"Really?"

"You bet," his dad said with a smile. "I can remember nights when you would cry and cry and cry and we had no idea what was buggin' you. Your mother never lost her temper, never once yelled or screamed. She would pat your back, sing in your ear, and pace back and forth on the floor all night long. Then, after you fell asleep on her shoulder, she would roll you onto her chest and sleep along with you. Lord, I tell you, it was when your mother was the most beautiful: asleep with you on her chest, a look of pure contentment and joy on her lips even though she was passed out cold."

"I wish I remembered her, Dad," George said, hanging his head.

"Hey, hey," his father said suddenly, lifting up George's chin and holding it in his hand. George's father had a sudden pain in his chest, for he ached to see his son so upset. "Don't you be sad, understand? Everybody loses somebody, that's part of life. You know I lost my old man when I was your age too."

"I know," George mumbled.

"But that's not what I'm getting at," his father continued. "I'm trying to tell you to cheer up cuz your mother told you to."

"Huh?"

"That's right," he said, suddenly smiling. "Your mother told me, no she insisted, with her last dying breaths that you were not to grow up sad. She loved you so much and she ached and cried over the fact that you would grow up without her. I think the only thing that kept her living for so long was the thought of you through those last days. She made sure that I told you all the goods things about her and not to focus on her death. That's why I never told you about it; that's why you heard the story first from your Aunt Patricia. Your mama wanted me to tell you only the good things."

"Wow!" George said, lifting his head up. "I just thought you never wanted to talk about it."

"Well, I don't," his dad answered. "But I woulda told you cuz she's your mom, even though it hurt me."

"Yeah, but I like talking about her, Dad, even though it hurts."

"Yeah, me too, son, me too," he said in a slow realization. "It's kinda funny. I always thought that it would hurt talking about your mom and all. Sitting here, talking about her with you, brings back all the good memories and good times we shared. It's like seeing her all over again."

"Tell me some more about her!" George said eagerly.

"Alright," his father answered.

They talked, laughed, and cried until the fire burned out completely and the first rays of sunshine began to show over the horizon. It was the best time George had ever had with his father. Finally, the last barriers were breaking between them. They could talk about anything now, not just the past. As the nights continued under the stars, George and his father talked about family, Ireland, religion, girls, and even politics once in awhile. They also had a few friendly arguments once or twice.

"What do you mean Joshua's a better fighter than David?" his dad said during a midday rest. They had been discussing the nightly wrestling matches between George's cousins David and Joshua back home in Boston.

"He is," George insisted. "He just eases up once in awhile when David plays a trick on him."

"You're crazy," his dad responded. "David uses his leverage and manages to throw Josh even though he's bigger."

"He's not using leverage," George argued. "He's catching Josh by surprise."

"I'll show you what using leverage is," his father grinned, suddenly jumping up and pouncing on George.

"Aaaaahhh," George whined and laughed simultaneously.

The two of them rolled around in the grass for several minutes. George's dad would get him in a hold every once in awhile, and each time George would manage to squeeze out of it.

"You're pretty good, son," his father said, panting and smiling at one point.

"You bet!" George yelled as he jumped at his father's leg and tripped him up. George's father was laughing so hard that he couldn't get any balance. George crawled onto his chest and tried to pin him. His father struggled, laughed, and then grabbed at George's back.

"Hold it right there!" a voice said suddenly.

George immediately stopped what he was doing and turned his head to look up. Standing above him, partially blocked by the noonday sun, was a boy not much older than George, pointing a shotgun at George and his dad.

"What are you doing on our claim?" the boy said menacingly.

"Your claim?" George's father said, slowly rolling out from under George so as not to upset the boy with the gun.

"That's right our claim," the boy said. "Didn't you see the stakes?"

"What stakes?" George said as he stood up and dusted himself off.

"Right over there," the boy said, waving his gun towards a small stake in the grass to his left.

"Uh...sorry we meant no harm," George's father said. "There ain't no need to point the gun at us."

"Who are you?" the boy grunted, still pointing the gun at their chests.

"We're travelers from Boston," George's dad said slowly. He felt extremely nervous with this boy who was obviously upset and maybe even a little eager to use his gun.

"Hey, we mean you no harm," George interrupted holding up his arms. "Look, we ain't even armed."

It was true. Although they had bought guns for the trip, both of the rifles they used were saddled with the horses.

"You're from Boston?" the boy repeated, ignoring George's comment.

"Yeah,"

"Then you must be one of those darn abolitionists," the boy said angrily. "You come here to cause more trouble?"

"No, we ain't abolitionists," George's dad said quickly. "And we certainly aren't here to cause trouble."

"We're on our way to visit my uncle in Lawrence," George added. Things were getting out of hand, so they had to do something before this boy went crazy.

"Lawrence is where all the abolitionists live!" the boy said through clenched teeth, stepping forward and squinting his eyes as he looked them over.

"Oooooohhhh," George said as he fainted toward the ground. The boy swung his gun to the left as he turned to look at George. George's dad quickly grabbed the gun and tossed it into his son's arms.

"Good work, son," his father said, aiming the gun now towards the boy.

"Thanks, Dad," George said smiling as he stood up again next to his dad.

Pow! A shot rang out over their heads.

"Put your hands up!" a voice called from behind them.

George's father sighed and dropped the gun, raising both hands in the air. George did the same. The boy then leaned down to pick up the gun lying in the grass.

"They're abolitionists, Pa," he called to the figure walking towards them. "I caught them on our claim and they took my gun!"

George turned his head to see an older man walking through the grass and wearing a dark hat with his gun pointed at their backs.

"That true?" the man said to George's father.

"Not really, sir," Sean answered, his hands remaining up in the air. "My son and I were simply stopping for a rest on our way to Lawrence when your boy surprised us and started threatening us with his gun."

"I didn't threaten you!" the boy yelled. "You wuz on our claim!"

"We were simply stopping for a rest," George's dad continued. "If you had let me explain instead of jumping to conclusions we never would have had any trouble."

"Look," the man interrupted, walking up to his son and pushing the gun downward. "We don't want any trouble, mister, but you never can tell in the territory just what's going on or who you can trust. What with no real law and all, anyone can take what they want out here on the prairie."

"All we want is to get to Lawrence," George's dad said.

"Lawrence is where all them abolitionists live, Dad!" the boy said.

"That's true, son, but just because they're abolitionists don't mean they're here to harm us."

"Yeah, but they took my gun," the boy persisted. "And they're traveling alone without any stuff to settle with. I bet they're raiders like old Brown."

"We're not raiders," George's father said quickly. He was losing his patience and was looking for a way out of this mess. "We're going for a visit. Look, there's a letter in my bag from my nephew's grandfather telling the people we're visiting all about why we're coming and what's going on. Come and take a look."

The man and his son slowly followed George's father keeping their eyes on them all the time. When they got to the horses, George's dad reached into the bag on his saddle, pulled out an envelope, and opened it.

"Here," he said handing it to the man.

The man cast his eyes down on the letter and began to read it very slowly. It was obvious that he was not used to reading because he would reread several portions at a time. His son continued to point his gun at George and his father while the two of them waited patiently for the man to finish reading.

"Look, I apologize," the man finally said when he finished reading. "It's just that with all the fighting between the abolitionists and the Missourians it ain't too safe around here. Hell, back in the spring, a buncha free staters were rounded up by some boys from Missouri or somewheres and they was all shot to death cuz they were against slavery. You musta heard about it."

"Yeah, I did," George's dad answered. "I think it was called the Marais Des Cygnes Massacre."

"Sure was," the man agreed. "And people are still talking about it. But heck, all we want is to start a new life here in Kansas, not to get involved in any political thing. We're gonna play it safe and not upset anyone on either side. So, how about if we help you on your way and we won't discuss this no more."

"Sure, that would be great," George's father said. "We were beginning to get a little lost anyway. We could use all the help we can getting to Lawrence."

"But Pa," the boy whined.

"Hush up, boy," he scolded him. "They're travelers like most folks. Let's show them a little hospitality, and then we can come back to finish laying out the claim."

Lawrence, Kansas

Watkins Community Museum of History, Lawrence, Kansas

Chapter 6
Lawrence, Kansas

"So, where are you from?" George said to the boy after the two of them had ridden a little ahead. Their fathers traveled behind them about 50 yards, riding slowly and calmly. They seemed content to allow the boys to go ahead.

"Illinois," the boy answered.

"Oh," George said awkwardly, sensing the boy did not quite trust him. They rode in silence a little longer.

"My dad's looking to start all over again," the boy suddenly began. "We weren't doing very well out near Springfield, so he decided to pack up the whole family and head off to Kansas."

"The whole family?" George asked.

"My ma and sister are still back home," the boy answered. "Dad felt that it would be better if he and I went first."

"Yeah, I can see why," George said. "Oh, by the way, my name is George."

"Charles," the boy responded in a soft voice.

They rode along some more in silence. The wind blew. The birds sang. A fox darted across the prairie.

"Why's your uncle in Lawrence?" Charles said, breaking the silence again.

"Uh...well," George began. He did not want to tell Charles too much, knowing how he felt about abolitionists. "He and my Aunt Regina went to help make Kansas a free state."

"They're free staters?" Charles asked.

"Yeah," George replied. "They left about two years ago. They had heard about the Emigrant Aid Society in Massachusetts looking for more people to settle the town. It wanted enough voters to make Kansas a free state, not a slave state. My uncle and aunt became involved with antislavery organizations, so when they found out that they were needed and would also get help moving they jumped at the chance."

"Sounds like they're abolitionists," Charles said accusingly.

"Well, sort of," George admitted. He knew that his uncle and aunt, who were very avid abolitionists, had helped fugitive slaves escape into freedom in the past.

"What do you mean sort of?"

"Well, they were against slavery," George explained. "But they were not the kind of people to cause the trouble you talk about."

"Hmph," Charles puffed. "Well, even if you're telling the truth, since they live in Lawrence they've already caused trouble."

"What do you mean?" George asked.

"You heard about the riots, didn't you?"

"Yeah," George answered. "Lots of pro-slavery guys rode into town, burned a bunch of buildings, and made a lot of noise, but no one was killed and my aunt and uncle wrote that they were fine."

"That may be true," Charles continued. "But if they hadn't rushed to Kansas to make sure it was free, then those pro-slavery men wouldn't have been so angry."

"Those pro-slavery men did not live here in the K.T.," Charles' father suddenly said from behind. The two men had ridden up to the boys a few minutes ago and had been listening quietly. "They had crossed the border from Missouri."

"I know that, Pa," Charles said. "But just the same, the people in Lawrence were asking for trouble when they came down in such a rush and started spouting off all their ideas."

"They got as much right as we do being here," his father answered.

"Yeah, but if it wasn't for them," Charles shot back, "we wouldn't have to worry so much about our property or our lives here in K.T."

"I've told you, son," his father began slowly, "that both sides in this stupid fight have pulled dirty tricks. The Missourians started the whole thing with that bogus vote, and the abolitionists made it worse with their second government."

"I don't understand," George interrupted. "If you two aren't free staters or pro-slavery men, how come you're here in the first place?"

"Not everyone's a politician," Charles answered. He was surprised and annoyed at George's question. "In fact, most people here just wanna start a new life. It's only because you read about the troublemakers in the papers that you think that way."

"That's right," Charles' father added. "I never really cared either way what happened. I'm probably against slavery cuz of what it would do to the economy, but I ain't going to burn no house or shoot no people on account of it."

"Sounds to me like you wanna be left alone," George's dad said.

"That's right," he agreed. "That's why we were so nervous when you showed up. We thought you were another ruffian, who had come to grab our claim or steal something."

"No, we're much like yourselves," George's dad answered. "We wanna be left alone too. We're on our way to Lawrence because we have to find my nephew. After that, we're headed on out."

The statement surprised George. He hadn't thought about what would happen after they found David. The idea of returning home depressed him.

"Dad," George suddenly said, "I don't wanna go back to Boston."

"Oh?" his father replied.

"Yeah," George went on. "It's so stuffy there. I can never do what I want; people are always making fun of us because we're Irish; and you gotta work so hard that I don't ever see you. Can't we go somewhere else or stay here on the prairie?"

"Hhhmmm," George's father answered. "Wow, I never thought of that, son. When your grandpa sent us here I just assumed we'd go back, but I guess we don't really have to."

"That's right, Dad!" George quickly stated. "We could become settlers ourselves and start a whole new life, just you and me."

"Hey, sounds exciting, doesn't it?" his father grinned. "I don't know. Maybe, we'll see."

George knew not to press his dad any further. It didn't make any sense anyhow with them having to go to Lawrence first. Maybe, once they completed their mission he would bring it up again.

As they rode in silence for a few minutes longer, George began to wonder when they would finally reach Lawrence. The prairie seemed to go on forever without the sight of any house or building, much less an entire town.

"There it is!" Charles suddenly called out.

"What?" George said looking around. As far as he could tell, everything still looked the same.

"The town! Don't you see it?" Charles answered.

"See what?"

"Look, straight ahead," Charles said pointing. "You see that steeple from the church and the smoke from the furnaces."

George squinted. "Oh yeah," he said.

"And to the left of the steeple," Charles continued, "is Mount Oread. You can even see the top of the few houses on it."

"There's a mountain there?"

"No, not a real mountain," Charles answered. "They call it that because it's as close to a mountain as you get here in K.T."

"Oh," George returned.

They rode a little longer and yet the town seemed no closer. The views on the flat plains completely confused George. He could identify the buildings and houses from a distance, but without roads, signs, or even a few stores along the way there certainly were no real signs that they were getting closer. Then, suddenly, the city popped out of the prairie, and they were now riding into Lawrence, headed for his Uncle John's store.

"Where's the store?" Charles' father, Abe, asked.

"Massachusetts Street," Sean answered.

"Yeah, well, that figures," Abe replied. "Everything seems to be on that street."

"Are we close?" Sean asked.

"Everything's close in Lawrence," Abe answered smartly. "But yeah, we head straight up that main street there."

George looked to where Charles' father was pointing. It seemed that the whole city was neatly laid out. It was nothing like Boston, George thought. Boston had been spread out all over the place with streets going in every direction and sometimes leading nowhere. The houses and buildings were crammed in tight. Even the people sometimes seemed as though they too had been forced into places in the street where they didn't want to be.

The city of Lawrence appeared to be wide open, much the same as the prairie. The wind swept through the streets, the birds flew overhead, and the smell of wildflowers floated in the breeze. Occasionally, a wild animal would dart down the street.

The organized, unpaved city streets were laid out with one set of streets heading in one direction while the other set crossed them perfectly, separating the land into neat blocks and making it easy to find your way.

The group turned the corner onto Massachusetts Street and instantly George knew that he was in the heart of the city. Activity filled the streets—people going about their business as they walked along or across the streets; horses were either tied to rail posts or trotted along with riders; shouts and laughter came from a saloon; and at one point a stagecoach roared by.

The buildings of various shapes and sizes appeared to be well built. There was the beautiful hotel with the typical saloons and stores and the familiar post office. George also noticed a bridge extending across a river with a steamboat making its way.

"Wow, you'd never know we were out in the open prairie five minutes ago," George said to no one in particular.

"Yeah," Charles agreed, "I'll say one thing for these Yankees, they sure know how to work."

"In a way it reminds me of Boston with all the rushing about and energy," said Sean.

"Yeah, but not that much, Dad," George added. "I don't ever think I've seen a street this wide in Boston."

"Or this dusty," his father answered as he coughed several times and waved the dirt from his face. "Are we almost there, Abe?"

"Right up there on the right," Abe answered. "Do you mind if Charles and I join you? We need some provisions for tonight anyhow."

"You're welcome to," Sean answered.

The four riders pulled their horses up next to the store and dismounted.

"You nervous, Dad?" George asked as he tied his horse's reins to the side post.

"A little," Sean replied quietly. "It's been over two years since I've seen my brother and he didn't leave on the best of terms."

"Were you angry at him for leaving his kids with you?" George asked abruptly. He and his father had never discussed how they felt about the fact that George's uncle had left his four children with them in Boston so he could move to Kansas.

"Well, sure I was," Sean answered as he approached the door to the store. "But that was a long time ago and I don't want to think about that now. Let's get this over with."

They walked into the store and looked around at the assortment of items everywhere: butter, eggs, apples, melons, chairs, tools, buckets, plates, whiskey, spoons, boots, and hats too. Every item that George could possibly imagine he could ever want and many he couldn't imagine filled the shelves. Some things were lying on the floor or crouched in a corner as though it had no particular place or space of its own.

"Hello there," a man dressed in simple blue overalls said as he turned around. "What can I do for you..., Sean?" he said with a look of shock on his face.

"Hiya, John," Sean said with a wave of his hand. "How ya been?"

"Sean, my God, Sean!" his brother yelled as he ran forward and grabbed him in a huge bear hug.

George awkwardly stood by as his father and uncle hugged. It had been a long time since he had seen his uncle and he could see changes in him. His face appeared harder and his eyes looked colder. A strange shiver went up George's spine.

"George!" Uncle John called out as his eyes caught George standing nearby. "Are you here too?"

"Hi, uncle," George said softly as he waved his hand.

"Look at you!" Uncle John exclaimed, breaking his hug with Sean and grabbing George. "You look more like your mother every day."

The statement put a sudden chill in the air as everyone was reminded that George's mother was dead. Uncle John took a step back, realizing he had said something awkward and quickly changed the subject.

"So," he began as he turned back to Sean, "what are you doing here, little brother?"

"I came for David," Sean answered.

"David?" John said as a puzzled look appeared on his face. "Why did you come for David?"

"Didn't he tell you?"

"Tell me what?"

"He is here, isn't he?" Sean asked in an attempt to put off the subject. He didn't want to get into the whole situation now.

"Yes," John answered. "He arrived over a month ago. What's this all about?"

"Where is he now?" Sean asked, ignoring his brother's question.

"He's in the back actually. Da-a-a-a-vid!" John called towards the back of the store. "Come on out here, will you?"

"What is it, Pa?" a voice called from the back. Noises could be heard of something being dropped or set down. Then George heard footsteps. Immediately, he became very upset as he realized that David was here, safe and sound, and totally unaware of everything he had put George through.

"Yeah, Pa, what is it?" David repeated as he appeared from behind the counter.

"Uncle Sean!" he shouted as he realized who was standing in front of him. He looked to the right. "George!"

Suddenly, his face was smashed to the side as a fist pounded his cheek. Blood spurted through his teeth and his body was thrown backwards.

"You son of a ——!" George yelled as he let another punch fly. All of the rage and embarrassment he had been holding inside of him was unleashed on David. How could he have left George behind in their grandfather's house when it was his idea to go there in the first place? How dare he take off to Kansas without a word of good-bye? How dare he act as though nothing had happened?

"Hey, hey, stop it, George, stop it!" David mumbled through the blood in his mouth. "What's the matter with you?"

"You left me all alone!" George yelled as he punched David in the stomach. "And I had to take all the blame for what you did, you son of a ——!"

George punched again, but this time David had finally managed to get his balance and held George with his greater size. He pushed him back a little and the two started to wrestle.

"Cut it out!" George yelled in frustration when he realized David was fighting back.

"Not until you do!" David yelled.

The two struggled, slipping, falling, and knocking down cans piled next to the counter.

"That's enough, you two," George's father said as he grabbed George by the back of the shirt and pulled him off David. "You're going to ruin the whole store."

"Will someone please tell me what this is all about?" Uncle John gasped.

Everyone looked at him in silence. No one wanted to be the first to speak and they all were unsure where to begin.

"Uh, excuse me," Abe suddenly interrupted. He and Charles, who had stood off in a corner quietly watching the whole thing, had been almost forgotten by Sean and George. "I think that maybe you folks need some privacy. So if you don't mind, Charles and I will go to another store."

"No, no wait," Uncle John said as he shook himself out of his confusion. "We can talk after you leave. What can I help you with, Mr....?"

"Bishop," Abe replied, putting out his hand. "The name's Abe Bishop."

"He and his son found us out on the prairie," Sean interrupted, his hand still gripping the back of the squirming George. "And they helped us find the city."

"Well, that's real nice of you," John said, straightening up his shirt and becoming businesslike. "So what can I do for you folks?"

"Well," Abe said slowly, looking at Sean. He felt uncomfortable with shopping after the brawl. "We need all kinds of things for several days of camping."

As John and Abe began to discuss all the provisions they would need, George's father pulled George and David to the side.

"You boys need to work things out," he began in a whisper, "after all that's happened. Why don't you take Charles with you and go outside while I help John and Abe."

David and George both stared angrily at each other.

"Charles," Sean said turning towards him, "you make sure these two don't fight. They used to be best friends and I'd like to see them like that again."

The boys all looked up at him.

"You gonna behave?" Sean asked his son.

"Yeah, Dad," George replied slowly.

"Good," he said, turning around and heading towards Abe and John who were talking. "Now, you boys go outside. I'll get you in a minute."

The boys went outside and sat near the horses. The street with all the traffic was noisy and dusty, but David didn't seem to mind as he wiped the blood from his cheek and sat close to George.

"I'm real sorry, George," he began. "I never meant to leave you all alone. I didn't know what to do when Grandpa came into the room."

"I know, I know," George answered. He felt exhausted, but good. A huge weight had suddenly been taken away from him now that he finally had confronted David. The anger as well as the sadness and frustration were gone. It was amazing what one good fight could do.

"I guess I needed to release some steam," George continued. "You had me pretty angry."

"Well, you certainly had some steam alright," David said rubbing his cheek again. "I think you knocked out two teeth."

"Sorry," George said slowly.

"Hey don't worry about it," David said quickly. "I guess I did have it coming to me. Who's your friend?"

"Oh, this is Charles," George said, turning and pointing towards Charles. "He and his dad are moving here from Illinois."

"Hiya," David said with a wave. "Welcome to Lawrence."

"Thanks," Charles said quietly. He felt very awkward with the two boys. It was obvious that they were close and Charles felt as though he was in the way. "But do you guys need me to go somewhere so you can be alone?"

"No, no!" George said quickly. "Don't worry about us. We don't need to talk nothin' out like my dad said."

"Yeah," David agreed. "George did all his talking with his fist and I think I got the message."

George laughed.

Charles laughed too.

"Hey, David," George said suddenly. "You got a baseball?"

"Baseball?" Charles asked. "What's a baseball?"

"Oh, come on," George replied. "You ain't heard of a baseball?"

"Well, I might have," Charles said cautiously. He was a little embarrassed because he didn't know what a baseball was.

"Yeah, I still got one," David answered. "But I haven't had much time to use it."

"That's great!" George answered. "Maybe the three of us could pass it around."

"Hey, that's a great idea," David answered. "There's hardly anyone here my age to play with and they're always too busy most of the time anyway."

"I don't know if I can," Charles said.

"Don't worry, it's easy," George said enthusiastically. He hadn't played since they had left Boston. "David will show you. Back home he was the home run king!"

"Home run?" Charles asked.

"Wow," George said. "I guess you have never heard of baseball, have you?"

"Well, I think my dad talked about it once," Charles began. "He had said it was one of those games they played back East."

"Yeah, it is," David said. "It's really popular in New York and Massachusetts; they even got some professional teams you can go to watch."

"Sounds neat," Charles replied. "But I don't know if I can—"

"Oh, come on, Charles," George said. "You'll love it!"

Suddenly the door of the store opened.

"Charles," his father said, "I need your help in here."

"Oooohhhhh," the boys all whined together.

"Alright, Dad," Charles said disappointed. He was looking forward to learning that game.

"We'll play soon, I promise," George yelled to him as he walked into the store.

"O.K.," Charles said waving. "See ya later."

"Bye," David and George said together.

The door closed behind Charles, leaving David and George standing alone on the street.

Chapter 7
The Explanation

"C'mon, boys, it's time to go home and get this whole mess sorted out," Uncle John said, opening the door and stepping out into the street. "I'm still waiting to hear just what this is all about."

"Coming!" David and George replied flatly, standing up and wiping off their dusty pants. The two boys exchanged nervous glances as they walked to join their fathers. They knew that they were in big trouble now and that they would have to explain the whole mess to David's dad and mother. It wasn't going to be easy, they realized, especially after the fight they had in front of everyone in the store.

Walking in silence, the two boys found Massachusetts Street a pleasant distraction. With its many shops, travelers, shoppers, and workers there was much to see and listen to. However, when they turned right and headed toward Rhode Island Street, the noises quickly faded. David and George were wondering what they would say and how their fathers would react. George was not that worried because his father already knew just about everything. Whatever he hadn't already learned the night of the robbery, George had told him on the trip west. David, on the other hand, had plainly lied to his parents. He had contrived some story about needing to get information for Grampa and had hoped that his parents would be so happy to see him that they would not question him too much; and they hadn't, at least until now, David thought.

As they traveled away from the town center and approached David's house, George marveled at the open spaces between the houses. He compared these spread-out buildings to those on Massachusetts Street and the neighboring streets where the houses and stores had been built right next to each other. David's house, a five- to ten-minute walk from the town center, stood alone on the street, waiting for other houses to join it. The nearest home was perhaps one hundred feet away. Uncle John had remarked that he did not expect to get another neighbor for several months to a year.

Uncle John knocked lightly on the door.

"Don't you have a key?" his brother, Sean, asked.

"Of course not," John replied with a laugh. "No one in the K.T. has a lock on their door. I'm knocking because I don't want to wake Regina."

"She's asleep?" Sean said puzzled. He looked around a little in confusion not sure why she would be asleep in the middle of the day.

"Well, she might be," Uncle John answered softly. "She's been real sick lately and I've been terribly worried. Some days she's fine, working and slaving like she's done since we arrived, and other days she's light-headed and weak. That's why she hasn't written to you in so long. She's been so busy catching up with our chores and not wanting to talk about how she feels that she kinda forgot to write for awhile."

"Yeah, we had been wondering," Sean replied. "In fact, that's mostly the reason for us being here as any other. Her father wanted us to check up on you guys."

"Well, that figures," Uncle John replied as he opened the door slightly. "William never did like the idea of us going out here by ourselves."

"No one did," Sean said as he followed his brother into the house. He was about to continue letting John know how much everyone had hated the fact that the two of them had left Boston and their children to go off on some abolitionist crusade. He was stopped only by the sight of David's mother, Regina, leaning sideways against the wall with her head propped up by the windowsill.

"Regina?" David's father whispered softly, not sure if she actually had fallen asleep in that position.

"John?" she said suddenly, startled out of her daze and turning around to greet him. "I didn't hear you come in."

"She has a little trouble with her hearing," Uncle John whispered behind him to the others.

"Don't worry about it, dear," he continued, turning back towards her and ignoring the fact that she may have been asleep. "I've got a surprise for you."

"S-Sean, G-George!" Regina stuttered as she saw the two visitors step into the room.

"Hello, Regina," Sean greeted her.

"Hi, Aunt Reg!" George called. He truly was happy to see her. He had not realized along the trip how much he had missed her because he had been so preoccupied with thinking about David. As he ran to hug her, he remembered how she had always made him laugh and treated him like her own son. Indeed, when George's real mother had died, Regina had taken it upon herself to fill that empty space in George's life by making him feel loved and wanted as only a mother could.

"George!" Regina called again as she extended her arms for a big hug.

The two hugged and laughed together for several moments as everyone else looked on and smiled. Suddenly, all the other concerns of the money, Grampa, Regina's health, and the troubles in K.T. all seemed to melt away in this brief moment of comfort and love. They were a family again.

"My God, George, I've missed you," Regina cried through tears as she pushed George backward a little to stare at him. "Look at you! You're so grown up. When I last saw you, you stood only up to my chest and now you're almost as tall as I am!"

George smiled broadly and turned to look back at his dad.

"See, I told you that I was getting bigger," he grinned.

"I never said you weren't," his father answered.

"Sean, look at you!" Regina said as she turned her attention to her brother-in-law. "You're even more handsome than I remember."

Sean blushed as he walked toward Regina to give her a big Irish hug.

"You always did know how to brighten up a room," he said grinning. "God, how we've missed you two."

"Well, you can't imagine how we've missed you," Regina answered as she pulled a chair out from the kitchen table and slowly sat down. "It's been pretty lonely here in the K.T., especially compared to when we lived with all of you in such a big family. There have been days when I've been so lonely for a good old family dinner that I've actually imagined I heard everyone's voices laughing, joking, and talking about old times."

"It hasn't been the same at dinner since you left," Sean said as he sat in the chair nearest to Regina.

"Yeah," George added quickly as he too sat next to his aunt. "Now Joshua and Zachary get their way a lot more and Uncle Robert makes the rest of us feel like his kids are more important because they work while we go to school."

"That doesn't surprise me," Regina whispered softly. "He always did give me a hard time for sending all of you to school. But no matter, as long as you remain in school and continue your studies he can ridicule you all he wants. Remember, he's simply jealous because somewhere deep inside him he realizes that someday you will be more important than his own children and that makes him afraid."

"Regina, we don't have time for this now," Uncle John suddenly interrupted. "Sean has told me that he has come for David and I want to know why."

"Come for David?" Regina repeated as she looked at Sean quizzically. "Why have you come for David?"

"Well, Reg," Sean began slowly, "it's a long story, but suffice it to say we came for David to get the money he stole from your father."

"Stole? David?" Regina gasped. "My son stole money from my own father? How is this possible?"

"Wait, mom, wait!" David quickly interrupted. "It's not like it sounds. I can explain!"

"It had better be good!" his father said sternly.

"Uhhhmm, well," David began slowly, looking nervously away from his father and at his mother. He didn't want another beating like the one his Uncle Robert had once given him. His father was even meaner than Uncle Robert when he got really angry.

"I was only doing what you would have done," David said meekly.

"What we would have done?" both his parents repeated in voices mixed with anger and confusion.

"Yeah," David answered. He was beginning to gather a little more courage. "You see, it was all for an escaped slave who had made her way up to Boston."

"What were you doing with an escaped slave?" David's father asked angrily.

"John, let me take over or we'll be here all night," David's Uncle Sean interrupted. "David and George had come across this escaped slave named Lisa who had nowhere else to hide because some slave catchers had already seen her in the city. They took her to our house where I said she could stay for awhile, but when our dear older brother, Robert, discovered her, he made her leave. David who insisted on helping her was unable to hide her from the slave catchers. David put up a brave fight but he got hurt, and the catchers managed to grab the slave and take her away."

"That's right," David jumped in. He felt really good now after listening to his Uncle Sean explain the whole situation. The way that his uncle told the story made David sound pretty noble. He never realized that his Uncle Sean might actually respect what he had done.

"So, after I watched her boat leave Boston Harbor and begin to sail south," David continued the story, "I didn't know what else to do. I asked Grampa for help but he was too busy. So at that point I got the idea of borrowing some money from him to come here. I knew that you would know what to do."

"Don't forget to tell them that you ran away with the money and left me to get in trouble," George added angrily.

"My God that's incredible," Regina said, ignoring George's comment. "But, David, why did you not tell us this? You've been here over a month."

"I didn't want to upset you with you being so sick and all," David answered apologetically.

"I am not sick!" Regina shouted in frustration. "I am just a little tired! Anyone would be if they worked as hard as I do."

"Of course you're not sick," Regina's husband, John, said tenderly, rubbing her shoulders and holding her hand. "David and I get worried whenever you're not your energetic self."

"Oohhhh," Regina sighed in a big breath. "I suppose it's only natural. But it's still no excuse for not telling us, David."

"I'm sorry, Mother," David replied. "I was only trying to help."

"I know you were, dear," Regina answered softly. "But trying to help does not mean you can go ahead and steal from your own Grandfather. You could have been hurt, or even killed, traveling all the way here by yourself."

"And," David's father added, "that money you stole was not yours and for all you know it may have been set aside for something even more important."

"Huh?" David said, not quite understanding John's last remark. David and the others in the room looked at him in a puzzled stare.

"Is there any money left?" David's father continued, ignoring the stares.

"Yeah, a little," David answered.

"Where is it?"

"I've been keeping it under my pillow."

"Go get it, please," David's father said sternly.

David turned and left the room while his mother stared at her husband with a slight smile on her face.

"It is our own fault, you know," she said to him with a smile.

"Maybe," he shrugged.

"If we had not exposed him to all the abolitionist meetings and preachings this might have never happened," Regina continued.

"Maybe," John said again.

"But I can't help being a little proud of him too," she smiled.

"I suppose," John answered.

"Here it is," David called as he walked back into the room. In his hand was the leftover money, still in the original envelope and wrapped in the paper he had found it in. He handed it to his father.

"Oh, my God," David's father said as he looked at the envelope.

"What is it, John?" Regina asked.

"The envelope," he replied slowly. "It says 'Brown' on it."

"Oh, my God!" Regina gasped.

"Brown...what's Brown?" Uncle Sean asked.

"Not what, who," Regina answered.

"Who?" Uncle Sean repeated. "Who?...Oh, Mary, Mother of Jesus!"

"What? What?" George yelled. "Who's Brown?"

"John Brown is the most famous, bravest, crazy man in the K.T.," Regina answered him slowly. "He is the one who attacked and killed the pro-slavery men at a place called Pottawatomie in reaction to their raid on our city."

"Him?" David said. "Oh, no! He's crazy! He sliced those guys to pieces with his sword and got clean away with it! I remember hearing about it when we were in school!"

"He's not crazy," David's father interrupted, unfolding the paper around the money and looking it over while he spoke. "In fact, he's very brave. Those men had it coming and John Brown was the only one with the guts to do anything about these lawless slavery supporters."

"John, let's not have this discussion again in front of the children," Regina interrupted.

"But why would Grampa have money set aside for John Brown," George asked. He still did not understand the whole situation, or what his aunt and uncle were making known.

"That's none of your concern, George," his Uncle John answered quickly. He folded the paper and hid it in his pocket. "And don't speak of it to anyone again. Is that clear?"

"But—"

"Is that clear?" he repeated.

"Yes, sir," George said softly.

"And David," John said, turning again to his son, "you are going to have to find a way to replace the money that you've stolen and to return it to your grandfather."

"But what about Lisa?" David complained.

"Who?" asked his father.

"My friend, the escaped slave," David answered. "I was hoping you would help me find her again."

"Forget her," his father answered simply. "Your concern now is repaying that money."

"But—"

"No buts, young man," his father said. "You will find yourself another job and replace that money as soon as you can or I will give you the punishment you deserve for stealing it in the first place!"

"Okay, okay," David said, holding up his hands to signal his father to stop. "I understand."

Chapter 8
The Stranger

"Did you get it?" the man in the black trenchcoat asked David's father.

"Yes," John answered. He looked left and right, then locked the door to his store so that no one would disturb them. "He gave it to me immediately. He doesn't suspect a thing."

"Are you sure?" the man asked, taking off his hat and rubbing his hands through his jet black hair.

"Of course I'm sure," John replied angrily. "He's my son, isn't he?"

"A son you left behind in Boston so you could move here," the man said critically. "The kid may have changed more than you know. After all, he kept the money a secret from you until he was exposed by the other boy. Isn't that so?"

"Yes, I suppose so," John agreed slowly.

"Then, it's possible he knows too much," the man said, rubbing his thick mustache with his right hand and glaring intensely at David's father.

"I doubt it," John quickly replied. He didn't like what this man was hinting at. "And besides," he went on, "even if he did know, what could he do? He's only a kid."

"Just the same," the man went on, taking the money out of the envelope and counting it, "I think I'll keep an eye on him just to be sure. There's enough money left to set me up for awhile and I don't think your father-in-law will mind. Do you?"

David's father didn't answer. He thought about what was being said and about the whole mess he was now involved in. How did it get this crazy? He left David behind in the first place to protect him from things like this. Now, not only was David here in Lawrence with him, but he was now possibly as deeply involved as he was. What could he do?

"Just make sure you don't lay a hand on him," John said finally. "This may be for a great cause, but the boy is still my son and I won't let any harm come to him. Is that understood?"

"Sure, sure, John," the man agreed. "Don't worry about a thing. I'm just going to keep an eye on him."

Meanwhile, David did not suspect a thing. He was too busy working at the Eldridge Hotel doing odd jobs, cleaning the stables or the saloon, or anything else they would have him do. With the winter season getting close, David knew that soon the number of travelers would drop dramatically and he would have trouble finding work again, so he had to work that much harder.

George found that he also had to spend more time working. With David gone from the house most of the time and Regina still not feeling well, George had to do most of the chores. His father had decided to stay in Lawrence until David had raised the money, and winter had passed. They also had to help around Uncle John's store. Most of the time when George was working with his dad they continued to have great discussions and occasionally threw the baseball around.

"You're getting quite an arm there, son," Sean said to George one day after they had been throwing the ball for over an hour.

"Thanks, Dad," George responded. "But I'm getting kinda tired. Can we take a break?"

"Sure," Sean answered. "And I'll tell you what. Why don't we head into town and get something to drink?"

"Okay!" George shouted quickly. Whenever they went into town and spent a little money it was a welcomed treat. "Maybe we can even see David."

"Maybe," his father agreed as he started walking. "He's at the hotel today, isn't he?"

"Yeah," George answered, tossing the ball to his dad as they walked. "I think he's cleaning the stables."

George and his dad walked slowly down the dirt road, tossing the ball back and forth as they went. Once in awhile George would miss the ball and he'd have to walk back along the road in order to retrieve it. When they turned onto Massachusetts Street, it became too crowded to toss the ball anymore, so Sean stuck it in his pocket.

"That's enough for now, son," he said, pointing towards the hotel as he walked. "Let's go see David."

"O.K.," George agreed.

Approaching the hotel entrance, they abruptly turned right towards the stables. George looked forward to surprising David, so he snuck up ahead.

"Quiet, Dad!" George whispered with his finger to his lips. "I wanna see if we can surprise him. I think he's all alone today and...oh, my God!" George interrupted himself. He held out his hand to stop his father.

"What is it, George?" his father asked.

"That guy," George said pointing ahead, "he's the one who I saw messing in our hotel room when we were traveling on the National Road."

"What?" his father wondered. "How do you know?"

"I'd recognize that black coat and black hair anywhere," George said assuredly.

"What's he doing?" Sean said as he peered around the corner above George's head.

"He's standing there," George said. He looked around the stables again to see what the man might be doing. "He's not doing anything, just watching."

"What's he watching?" Sean said.

"I don't know," George answered. "He...wait!" George almost yelled. "He's watching David."

"David?" Sean repeated.

"Yeah," George explained. "David's over there in the corner. See him? The guy's watching David clean up."

"That's strange," Sean wondered aloud. "I wonder what he's up to?"

"Let's watch and find out," George suggested. "Then maybe we might be able to figure out why he was rummaging through our stuff in the first place."

"Good idea," Sean agreed.

Sean and George backed up a little to avoid being seen while they continued to watch the stranger. He never made a move towards David, but he continued to look around everywhere as if he was afraid of being found.

"I told you he's up to no good," George reminded his father. "Look at the way he's skulking about."

"I think you're right, son." Sean said. "We'd better keep an eye on him. There's no telling what he's doing."

When the manager came to talk to David the man stepped back into the shadows to hide. Then, when the coast was clear, he came back again.

"He's approaching David!" George almost shouted.

"Shhhh," Sean reminded him. "He'll hear us."

"Shouldn't we do something?" George asked as he began to stand.

"Not yet," his father replied, placing his hand on George's shoulder and sitting him back down. "He doesn't appear to have a gun, so let's see what he wants first."

George and Sean watched as the man approached David slowly. David appeared to be surprised by him but not afraid. The two exchanged words until the man began to yell.

"You're lying!" George could hear him shout at David.

"No," David yelled back.

The man grabbed David by the shirt and started throwing him back and forth.

"Dad!" George shouted to his father.

"Just one more minute," Sean said anxiously.

The man continued to push David. Struggling to break the man's grip, David managed to punch the man right in the jaw.

"You little...," the man shouted as he shoved David to the ground. "I'm going to make you pay for that!"

The man took out a long knife from his pocket. As he slowly made his way forward, David backed up on his hands and knees until he had nowhere to go—the man had cut off his escape.

"Dad!" George shouted.

Sean looked around and thought for a second before he reached into his pocket, pulled out the baseball, and whipped it as fast as he could.

"Aaaahhh," the man screamed as the ball hit him in the head. He stumbled backwards without falling to the ground. As the man turned to see where the ball had come from, Sean rushed in and punched him hard in the face. The man yelled stumbling backwards.

"Uncle Sean!" David yelled. "What are you doing here?"

"Back off, David," Sean yelled as he put up his fists to prepare for the man's counterattack.

"Who the heck are you?" the stranger growled as he wiped the blood from his jaw.

"The question is, who are you?" Sean countered.

As David and George looked on, the two men began circling each other. Neither one said a word as they held their fists in front of their faces and looked for an opening to strike.

The stranger threw a punch first. Sean blocked it easily. He threw another and another. Sean blocked both of them.

"That a way, Dad!" George yelled. He knew his dad was one of the best fighters in the neighborhood. More than once, Sean had come home from a bar fight with a broken nose or a bloody jaw, each time joking that the other guy was a lot worse off. "I know you can beat him!"

The stranger threw another punch. Sean blocked it again when he countered with a punch of his own. The stranger stumbled backwards as his nose began to bleed. Sean punched again and again. The man fell.

"Had enough?" Sean asked.

Without a word, the man wiped his nose and stood up again. His arms trembled in front of his face, and his legs wobbled. Sean punched once, twice, three times until the man fell down again. Sean stood over him smiling.

"Yeah, Dad!" George cheered.

David cheered too, but then the boys quickly froze in fright as the man pulled a gun out of his side holster and aimed it at Sean.

"Back off!" the stranger warned.

Sean nervously took a step back. The stranger stood up slowly, keeping his gun pointed at Sean.

"Don't shoot!" a voice cried out as a man ran in between Sean and the stranger. It was David's father, John.

"Dad!" David cried out.

"John!" Sean yelled to his brother. "Get out of the way!"

"No, Sean," his brother replied. "I know this man," John said, turning towards the stranger. "Harry, put the gun away!"

The stranger looked at David's father, then looked around. The gun didn't budge.

"I said put the gun away," John repeated.

Slowly, looking again from side to side, Harry put the gun back in its holster.

"I thought I told you to keep your hands off my son," John began.

"You know this guy?" Sean said in confusion.

"Yes," John answered apologetically, turning toward his brother. "He arrived shortly before you did."

"B-but," George interrupted, "I saw him in our hotel room a few months ago."

John looked at Harry waiting for him to offer an explanation.

"He must have ridden ahead of us," Sean guessed. "But what is he doing here and what does he want with us?"

"Don't say anything, John," the man spoke for the first time.

"Grandfather sent him," John explained, ignoring Harry's comment. "He was afraid that we wouldn't get the money back."

Everyone was quiet for a moment while they thought about John's comment.

"But," George said slowly as he thought out loud, "if he wanted the money, why is he still here?"

"He wants to know if we read the paper in the envelope," David answered. "That's what he was asking me about."

"What paper?" Sean asked.

"The paper that had a bunch of names and numbers on it, Dad," George explained. "The money was wrapped in it."

"John, what's this all about," Sean demanded.

When Harry began to protest, John quickly cut him off.

"I can't tell you that," John said boldly. "Trust me, it's none of your concern."

"I told you that they knew nothing," John said angrily. "But you insisted on causing all this trouble."

"I had to know for sure," Harry answered sheepishly.

"Well," John wondered, "are you satisfied now?"

Harry looked around again. Sean, George, and David were all standing, silently wondering what was going to happen next.

"I guess so," Harry finally answered.

"Then get the heck out of here, go back to Boston, and tell my father-in-law that everything is fine," John commanded.

Harry looked at the group again and thought about what had just been said.

"Go!" John shouted.

"Alright," Harry replied as he turned away to leave. "But you just remember what this is all about."

"I won't forget," John answered.

Chapter 9
Dads

John never did explain to anyone what was going on and David didn't press his father. He wanted to get along with him now that they were no longer in the city. Everyone was used to John keeping secrets and doing strange things in the middle of the night. Indeed, for as long as David and George could remember, John had been secretive and mysterious. They had learned not to press him with any questions as he would get angry and storm out of the room. Generally, they all knew it had something to do with escaped slaves and abolitionism. They grew tired of asking and tired of wondering.

"That's the way he is," David said to George.

The boys went on doing their chores and playing when they could. Many times, they visited with their new friend, Charles, from the prairie. He and his dad had finished staking their claim and had quickly built their house. Even though there were even more chores for Charles and his dad to do, David and George were able to get some free time once in awhile to ride out to Charles' house to hang out on the prairie. They would play cowboys and Indians, or throw rocks at all the animals scurrying around.

The best times occurred when Charles and his dad would go into town to play a game of baseball with David, George, and their fathers. Most of the time the fathers were too busy with their chores; however, on a rare Saturday or Sunday when the weather permitted and the chores were completed, all six of them would walk onto a clear section of the prairie near the house and play a father and son baseball game.

"C'mon, strike him out!" Sean yelled to his brother, John, on a brisk December morning. "Whatsa matter, you afraid to pitch it hard on your own son?"

John grinned and stared from the pitcher's mound at his son, David. Studying his father carefully, David gripped the bat tighter. Every ball his father had thrown to him was low and to the inside. David wondered why his father was pitching all of them the same way today, for he could easily pitch it high and outside. Looking at his dad's eyes again, David suddenly realized his father had been setting him up. The next pitch would be high and to the outside.

"C'mon John!" Charles' father, Abe, shouted as well. "The kid's already had three homers today!"

"And he'll get another one!" Charles yelled from his safe spot at third base. After only two or three lessons Charles had become an excellent hitter as well, for this was already the fourth time today he had gotten on base. "C'mon, David, hit me home!"

David gripped the bat even tighter. His father wound up. The ball came sailing high, exactly where David knew it would.

"C-c-crack!" the bat smashed the ball high into the air.

"Yeah!" George shouted from his spot behind the plate. "Way to go, David! Run, Charles, run!"

Charles and David raced along the baselines.

Uncle Sean raced beyond the outfield to find the ball.

"Run, Sean, run!" his brother called from home plate. "Throw it to me before he gets home!"

David rounded second and looked to see his Uncle Sean grabbing the ball and tossing it forward. It still had a way to go when Charles' dad caught it. At that point David rounded third.

"Throw it, Abe, throw it!" John called.

"Run!" George and Charles yelled to David from behind the plate.

David raced towards home where his dad was waiting for him. The ball came sailing over David's head. His dad caught it and grinned.

"Oh no!" David said as he realized he'd been caught. He turned around to head back to third.

The ball zipped over his head again and landed in Abe's glove who had run back to third.

"Oh no," David said as he again turned and headed back towards home. The ball sailed over his head yet again. His father was coming closer. David ran back.

The action continued for several seconds. Each time David would turn, one of the fathers would throw the ball towards his destination, and each time the ball was thrown the two fathers took a few steps closer to David. All three were beginning to laugh as David ran faster and faster and the space between the two ball throwers grew smaller and smaller.

Abe threw the ball again to John. David stared and smiled at his father. For one brief second his father stood motionless. Then, he held the ball high in his hands motioning a throw. David looked down.

Suddenly, he dove between his father's legs, taking him by surprise and coming out the other side. His father swung the ball down at David too late.

"Hey!" he yelled.

"Hah-hah," David taunted as he scrambled to his feet and stepped on home plate. "Now it's 8 to 2, our lead."

"Why you!" his father called as he rushed towards David.

David stumbled back laughing as his father approached until he was quickly taken by the much bigger, faster man.

"Stop it, stop it!" David yelled through giggles as his father tickled him everywhere.

"Say, 'My dad's a great pitcher first,'" David's father said as he continued to tickle him.

"No way!" David yelled back through his laughter.

"Say it!" he repeated, increasing the tickles and rolling David onto the dirt.

"O.K., O.K.," David called. "My dad's a great pitcher, my dad's a great pitcher!"

"Good," his father said, leaving David on the ground, as he stood up and clapped his hands back and forth. "I'm glad we got that settled. Now, let's finish the game."

George grabbed the bat and walked towards the plate while his Uncle John returned to the pitcher's mound.

"Hit another one, George!" David called as he dusted off his pants and looked over at his father with a smile. "He can't pitch!"

John looked back at his son, grinned and pretended to start running at David again. "Watch it!" he called through a smile. "Or I'll come after you again."

David giggled as he walked to where Charles was sitting.

"Your dad's a pretty fun guy," Charles said as David sat on the grass next to him.

"Yeah, thanks," David answered, realizing for the first time that Charles was right. His dad *was* pretty fun. He never did punish him for stealing the money and he never even yelled at him the entire time that David had been in the K.T. In fact, David thought to himself, his father had spent a lot of time with him throwing the baseball, walking him to his job, and just hanging out. A couple of times he would close the shop and walk over to David's job to spend lunch time with him.

"C'mon, pitch it!" George yelled as he swung the bat several times to warm up while his Uncle threw the ball to the other fathers. They would catch it and throw it back to show that they were ready for the next batter.

"Batter up!" George's dad called as he returned the ball to Uncle John.

Uncle John whipped a fast one right past George.

"Steeee-rike one!" George's dad called from first.

George growled at his father, picked up the ball, and returned it to his uncle.

Another pitch came whizzing by.

"Steee-rike two!" his father called again.

"C'mon, Dad, give him a chance!" David yelled.

His father looked at David then back at George. He grinned and tossed a slow, high pitch up in the air. It hung for so long that George got nervous waiting for it to come down.

C-c-c-crack! The ball sailed in the air over first plate. George laughed as his father turned around and ran for the ball.

"Run, George, run!" David and Charles yelled.

George easily ran the bases while his father kept after the ball. He rounded first, then second, and then saw his dad getting the ball.

"Keep going, George!" David yelled.

George rounded third as the ball came flying to the pitcher's mound. His Uncle John caught the ball without moving from his position.

George stepped on home plate.

"Yayyy!" all three boys yelled.

George turned and looked back at the pitcher who had never moved. Instead he had turned his attention away from the game staring off towards the street.

"Hey, Dad, what's wrong?" David asked.

"I've gotta go, son," he answered softly as he dropped the ball on the mound and walked away. "Something's come up."

"Hey, where's he going?" George asked.

"Yeah, you can't quit in the middle of an inning," Charles added.

"Shut up, you guys," David said bitterly. "Can't you see the sheriff waiting for him."

The other two boys looked at the sheriff who was standing near the street waiting for David's dad.

"What does Sam want with John?" Charles' father, Abe, asked as he and George's father walked toward the boys. "Is there trouble brewing?"

"Don't know," Sean answered. "But that ends the game."

"Ohhhhh," all three boys moaned. "Can't we still play?"

"C'mon, boys, you know that the sheriff is going to be busy with John for a while now," Sean said as he watched the two men walk away. "How can we pitch and field with only the two of us? Besides, you boys were creaming us anyway. Abe and I are gonna go down to the saloon and have a drink."

"Here," he continued as he reached into his pocket and pulled out a nickel. "Why don't you all run down to the bakery and get yourselves something?"

The game split up as Abe and Sean wandered off to the saloon while the boys headed down to the bakery. The nickel was more than enough for them to get some cookies or split a pie or something. Once there, they settled on some big oatmeal raisin cookies (which Charles never had eaten before) and headed down Massachusetts Street to the river.

"Wow, this is great," Charles said as he took another bite. "I can't believe I've never had these before."

"Doesn't your mom bake?" George asked.

"Sure she does," he answered. "But she's never used oatmeal before. In fact, I've never really had any 'til we got to Lawrence."

"There's nothing better than it on a cold morning, to warm you up and fill your belly," David said.

"Yeah," George agreed.

The boys walked some more in silence. The street was a little quieter now that many of the travelers were gone for the winter. There was plenty to look at though and they still could not walk right down the street without having to go around someone on a horse or in a carriage.

"Sure wish we could have finished the game," George said.

"Yeah, we were creaming them," Charles added. "How come your dad had to leave, David?"

"He's always in some mystery meeting," George answered for David.

Charles looked suspiciously at David. His skeptical questions of whether they were all abolitionist troublemakers started to return.

"What kind of meetings?" he asked.

"Nothing special," David answered. "And he doesn't go that often."

"Sure he does," George answered. "He disappears at least once a week. Sometimes he's even gone overnight. We all sit and wonder where he goes and—"

"Shut up!" David yelled. He still was upset that his father left the game. George was right that he always disappeared, leaving them all alone. David had wanted to go with him or at least know what he was doing, but his father always was mysterious and would never say a word about what he was doing. He would just go.

"Why do I have to stop talking?" George shot back. "It's your old man who ruined the game, not mine!"

"He didn't ruin the game!" David yelled.

"Sure he did! He's always ruining our fun. Every time we do something together he disappears for some meeting."

"He's got important things to do!"

"Like what?"

"I don't know, just stuff!"

"What's more important than being with your family?" George asked.

David stopped and looked back at George. He had nothing to say to that comment. Tears began to swell up in his eyes. He turned and ran.

"David, wait!" George called to him. "I'm sorry, I didn't mean—"

"Let him go," Charles said. "He needs to be alone."

Chapter 10
Regina

"W hy do we have to chop all this firewood?" Charles complained.

"Because we need it to last the whole winter," George answered as he placed another log on the chopping block. "And with Uncle John gone for over a week now we don't know when we'll get another chance to find more wood."

"Where did he go anyway?" Charles wondered aloud. The axe in his hands came crashing down smashing the log in half that George had put on the block.

"Who knows?" George answered. "Maybe it has to deal with all that trouble at Fort Scott. What do you think, David?"

"I don't know," David shrugged from the side of the house. He was picking up the chopped wood from George's pile and bringing it to a safe place alongside the house. In the dead of winter they would need all the wood they could get. Sometimes they would have to go quickly for more in the middle of the night or in the rain. It was important that the wood be close and easy to find.

"What do you mean you don't know," Charles said angrily. He was upset at having to stay behind when his father returned to Illinois. "My dad goes off and leaves me alone with you guys but at least he tells me everything. Whatsa matter, you afraid to talk to him or something?"

"Charles, you better watch what you're saying," George said cautiously. He could see that David was already getting upset.

"Why should I watch what I'm saying?" Charles shot back. "You afraid David's going to break?"

"No," George answered. "I was just saying that—"

"Shut up, George," David said angrily, dropping the wood he was carrying and pushing George to the side. "I don't need my little cousin protecting me from this loser."

"Loser?" Charles repeated. "Who are you calling a loser?"

"I'm calling you a loser," David shouted as he approached Charles and stood menacingly over him. David who was much bigger than Charles could easily take him in a fight, but before today he had always tried to keep his distance.

"I'm sick of hiding my feelings from you, and I'm sick of you judging us!" he continued, stepping even closer to Charles. "Ever since I met you I've felt like I had to hide what my parents felt and the kind of people they are. George told me how you felt about abolitionists, and you seemed like a nice kid, so I kept it all to myself but I'm sick of it."

"Hey, David," George interrupted, grabbing David's arm. "Leave him alone."

"No!" David shouted, swinging his arm out from George's grasp. "This kid has made me feel ashamed of my dad and my mom and I'm tired of it. I'm tired of the half-truths, the lies, and the funny stares he gives me."

"I don't give you funny stares," Charles argued.

"You do too," David responded. "Every time we mention my dad going to a meeting or my mom writing a letter, you give us these funny stares."

"So?" Charles asked with a confused look on his face.

"So it ticks me off!" David shouted, pushing Charles back in the chest. Charles stumbled backwards and fell on the ground.

"You sit there and think you're so much better than me," David said to the fallen Charles, his finger pointed down at him and his face red with fury. "You think that your dad is better and that my dad is some mystery guy who doesn't care about me."

Charles stared at him while George looked nervously from the side.

"Well, you're wrong!" David yelled, his voice beginning to shake. "You couldn't be more wrong. My dad does care about me! But he also cares about our country. While you and your old man worry about yourselves and your little claim, my dad is worried about the safety and well-being of our country and the millions of black people enslaved by them."

"Dayy-vid," George warned. "I don't know if you wanna say this."

"Of course I want to say it," David answered, ignoring the warning. "Charles needs to know that there's more to life than only himself. He judges my dad as a loser when he really is doing important things!"

"I knew it," Charles said starting to rise. "I knew your dad was involved in all kinds of illegal stuff. You're another one of those stinking abolitionists trying to cause trouble for the rest of us."

"You son of a ———," David shouted as he belted Charles in the face as soon as he was on his feet. "Who do you think you are?"

Charles stumbled back putting up his fists to defend himself.

"Stop it, you two!" George shouted. "Don't let that stupid stuff get in our way."

Ignoring George, the two boys began to circle.

"David, stop it," George yelled, grabbing his arm. David threw George back and turned to face Charles. A fist hit him in the face as Charles took advantage of the distraction to catch David off guard.

"Nice shot," David said, wiping the blood off his chin. "Let's see what you can do when I'm looking."

Again the boys circled, trading blows and dodging punches. David clearly had the advantage with his size and strength, but Charles managed to avoid him enough to land a few blows to David's stomach.

"Aunt Regina, Aunt Regina!" George called as he ran to the house. Normally, he would love to watch a good fight like the ones David and Josh used to have in the family room in Boston. But this one was different. This was real. George was afraid that this fight could end their friendship forever and he liked Charles and David too much to allow that to happen.

"What is it? What is it?" Aunt Regina cried as she opened the door. "Oh my God!"

"David!" she called as she ran to where the two boys were fighting. Charles turned and looked. David, ignoring his mother, leveled a deadly blow to Charles' face. He crumpled to the ground.

"What have you done?" David's mother screamed as she bent down to help Charles. His nose was bleeding uncontrollably as his hands tried to catch the flowing blood.

"My nose, my nose!" Charles cried through the blood. "He broke my nose."

"Serves you right," David said mercilessly.

"David Adams!" his mother said turning towards him after she had given Charles a handkerchief. "What in the Lord's name have you done?"

"I'm sorry, Mother," David apologized, realizing for the first time what had truly happened. "He got me so angry when he started making fun of dad and all."

"Why was he making fun of your father?" she asked.

"You know," David answered, "talking about how he's never around and going off to meetings and other stuff."

"And that gave you the right to break his nose?" his mother said angrily.

"No," David answered softly, bowing his head and looking at his feet.

"We'll talk about this more when your Uncle Sean gets back from the store," his mother answered, putting her arms under Charles and helping him up. "For now, help me get Charles in the house."

David and George helped Regina get Charles to his feet and lead him to the house where they laid him on a bed and began cleaning his nose. The anger had passed from everyone except for David's mother who seemed anxious and tired. She cleaned the blood off the floor and wiped Charles' face and David's hands with a wet rag.

"You boys," she began, "you're like the men, using your fists to solve all your problems."

The boys looked away in silence.

"Ever since we got to Lawrence all I've seen is violence," she continued. "The pro-slavery men attack us; then we go off to attack them. John Brown kills people in Missouri and is seen as a hero. The sheriff arrests people but nothing is done, and all the while I sit here and wonder why you men always have to fight."

"But mother," David began, "this is important. We're trying to free people."

"Don't you think I know that young man?" she scolded. "My God, after all the meetings I've attended, speeches I've listened to, and books I've read, don't you think I know exactly what is at stake here?"

David didn't answer.

"Don't you think I can see all the black people crying for help, their faces towards heaven and their hands in the dirt?" Regina paused a little to catch her breath and sat down on the bed next to Charles.

"I know that something has to be done boys," she said, looking at them deeply, her voice growing soft and her face etched with worry. "But I'm afraid at what may be done."

The boys all seemed confused.

"This is only the beginning," she explained. "The violence here in Kansas is only a taste of what is to come. If we don't find a way to quickly free the slaves legally with the Southerners' consent, we will have an awful war. North will fight South, brother will fight brother, and we will weep over the losses of our husbands and sons."

"My Lord, David," she cried, staring into his eyes as she caressed his cheek. "If war comes you will be one of the first to go."

She began to cry. Tears flowed freely down her face as she sobbed uncontrollably. David reached out to hug her tightly.

"I don't want to lose you," she sobbed. "I don't want to lose John; I don't want to lose everything and everyone I've ever known and loved."

"It's O.K., Mom, it's O.K.," David said trying to comfort her. Her sobs had turned to almost gasps for air as her chest began to heave up and down faster and faster.

"I've tried to stop them," she gasped. "I've tried to convince your father to try a different path but he doesn't listen! He's gone crazy with hatred; he's gone crazy with a desire to end slavery at all costs. You've got to stop him, David. You've got to make him see that there is another way. You've got to...ooohhhhh!"

Moaning in pain she collapsed in David's arms.

"Mother!" he cried. "Mother, what's wrong?"

"She's fainted!" Charles said. "Quick, get her some water."

The boys tried to comfort Regina by wiping her forehead and laying her down. Her face had grown very pale, and her breathing had become shallow.

"What's wrong?" George asked. "Why isn't she waking up?"

"This is more than a fainting spell," Charles added. "There's something wrong."

"What's going on here?" George's father said abruptly as he opened the door.

"Dad!" George called. "Thank God you're home."

"Regina," he cried, setting down his groceries and heading toward the bed. "What's wrong? What happened?"

"We don't know, Dad," George answered. "She was cleaning up Charles' nose after the fight and—"

"What fight?"

"Uhhhh, the fight David and Charles had," George answered uncomfortably.

"You boys had a fight in front of her?" Sean asked angrily.

"We didn't mean to," David said softly.

"Didn't you realize how this would upset her?" he scolded.

They didn't answer.

"She's still recovering," he continued. "And your fighting may have caused a setback for her!"

The boys all stared at one another.

"Well, don't just stand there like idiots," he scolded. "You started this thing, so do something about it! David, get some pillows to comfort your mother; Charles, you start a fire; and George, run to get a doctor. Hurry!"

The boys scampered to do what Sean had asked them to do, while he sat by Regina's side trying to comfort her. Shortly, George returned with the doctor who said there was nothing that he could do for her. They would just have to wait it out.

The days grew colder and darker as winter came on strong. There was no sign of David's father, and his mother's condition seemed no better. Once or twice she had woken from her fever, talking in mixed sentences which made no sense. As the calendar days changed from 1858 to 1859 and everyone was celebrating the New Year, David sat by his mother's bed wondering whether he would ever see either of his parents again.

Chapter 11
Ruffians

Spring had come. With the freshness in the air and the newness of the young flowers, David felt a renewed sense of hope. His father had returned safely from his adventure in southeastern Kansas, and his mother had recovered enough from her sickness that she could again speak and do some light chores. For awhile they even had some extra food that David's father had brought back with him until Regina found out how he got it.

Evidently, John had gone on a trip to Fort Scott to get some friends out of jail. They had been put there by an unpopular pro-slavery judge. While there, David's father decided to meet up again with John Brown on a raid into Missouri. They had ransacked several plantations, set some slaves free, and returned to Kansas as wanted men. No one was able to catch Old Brown, and the authorities were too busy with other things to even notice that David's dad was involved in the raid.

Regina had made John donate all the captured items to charity. He still felt extremely guilty at the fact that while he was away his wife had fallen into a deep sickness that she almost did not recover from. He promised to never leave her again and even tried to make amends to David by spending more time with him.

George managed to convince Charles to come back and hang out with them. Ever since the fight George had felt in the middle. He didn't really care about David's or Charles' politics. All he wanted was to play with them again. So, one day, he rode to Charles' newly finished house to apologize for David. Then, he went home to tell David that Charles had apologized. So far, neither boy had figured out what George had done. Once again, they were playing baseball and going to the bakery together for sweets.

One day, David's dad, John, announced that he was taking David, George, and his father, Sean, hunting. They had hunted before for food but never as a whole group. John said that they could possibly invite Charles since they could head in that direction for the game.

After saying good-bye to Regina and making sure that the doctor would check on her throughout the day, the two men and their sons set out on a hunting trip. David and George were given ordinary muskets. John and Sean were carrying the new, extremely accurate Sharp rifles.

"Whew, this sure is a nice gun," Sean said to his brother after they had left the house. Holding the gun by the butt and spinning it around, Sean noticed that it was not like the regular front-loading muskets that George and David were carrying, which seemed more bulky and inaccurate than this new beauty. This rifle, which had a smooth handcrafted end with a metal trigger and a shorter steel barrel for the bullet, was much quicker to load and more accurate to operate.

"Must be pretty expensive," he continued. "Where'd you get it?"

"It's one of those new back end-loading Sharps," John answered. "Shipments of 'em have been coming to Lawrence ever since I been here."

"They have," Sean asked. "How come?"

"I don't know," John replied. "It seems that we are always getting help from the aid society back in Boston. They send us all kinds of things and it's a good thing they do. What with all the problems we've had here, I don't know what we'd do without these little babies."

John rubbed the gun up and down with his hand.

"You ever shoot a man?" he said suddenly to his brother.

David and George suddenly looked up and started paying attention.

"No," Sean answered awkwardly. "You?"

"Once," John replied slowly. Now that the boys were paying attention he suddenly felt unsure of himself and did not want to discuss the topic anymore. "But it was in self-defense. This pro-slavery man was taking potshots at us and he woulda killed somebody soon. So I aimed and fired. Actually, I don't know whether I was the one who shot him. Me and a buncha guys all shot at the same time."

"Sounds rough," Sean said, not wanting to hear more details with George right next to him.

"Yeah, it was," John answered, trying to change the subject now. "But, uh...yeah, you were asking about the gun itself. It uh...sure is good for hunting. With those old ones the boys have, if you don't hit the critter with your first shot he's off, but with these new Sharps you sometimes have enough time to get off another shot if you're quick."

"Sounds great," Sean replied, relieved that the subject had been changed. "So, what are we looking for today."

"I don't know," John replied. "What do you boys wanna do?"

"Let's see if we can get something really big!" George said.

"Yeah, like a deer!" David added.

"Or maybe a wolf!" George continued.

"You don't hunt wolves," David scolded.

"Why not?" George asked.

"Because they usually roam in packs," David answered. "Besides, they don't taste no good anyhow."

"If you don't hunt them, how do you know they don't taste good?" George teased.

"Oh, cut it out, boys," George's father said. "We'll find what we can find. Just keep your mouths shut so we don't scare everything away for miles around."

The group walked for almost an hour away from the town. After leaving the city limits they passed into the prairie looking for game, but today nothing appeared. Heading in the general direction of Charles' house, John began to walk slower, keeping his eye on the ground.

"Whatcha doing, Dad?" David asked.

"Looking for tracks," he answered.

"Find any?"

"No, not yet," he replied. "But I'm sure we'll find something soon."

The group walked a little further in silence.

"Thanks for taking all of us," David said. "It sure is nice being together again."

"Yeah, it is," his father answered.

"Can we do this more often, Uncle John?" George asked.

"We haven't finished yet," Sean said.

"I know," George answered. "But I know I'm gonna have a good time. I always do when we're all together."

"Yeah, it's great," David said. "Just the fathers and sons, off on a hunting trip. What could be better?"

"Yeah," David's father laughed. "What could be better?"

"Hey, John, look at this," Sean suddenly interrupted, stopping where he stood and pointing to the ground. "These aren't game tracks."

"No," John answered, bending down for a better look. "They're horses, and there's a lot of them."

"Settlers perhaps?" Sean suggested.

"No, the tracks are too spread apart," John replied. "These horses were moving fast and weren't carrying much extra weight."

"Maybe the sheriff's gone out after someone!" George shouted.

"Sheriff's still in town," his uncle answered. "I saw him before we left. He told me all is quiet."

"Well, it's probably nothing serious," Sean said.

"No, but they may scare the game away," John replied.

"Well, let's turn this way," Sean said pointing.

They continued to walk along the grasses. George and David became depressed because no big game had come their way. Once or twice a jackrabbit came close enough, but neither George nor David were good enough marksmen to get the bunnies on such short notice. When they were getting close to the Bishop's house they picked up the pace only stopping when they thought a large animal might be nearby.

"Hey, look," George called from his position up ahead. "More tracks."

"They look like the same ones," his father said as he caught up to where George was pointing.

"They sure are," David's father said. "No wonder we haven't seen much game. These guys passed through here a little while ago probably scaring all the game around for miles."

"Hey, look!" David yelled, pointing into the sky. "What's that?"

"Looks like smoke," Uncle Sean said.

"Hey, isn't that where Charles lives?" George exclaimed.

"My God, it is!" David agreed. "We gotta help him! C'mon!"

David and George bolted through the tall grasses with their fathers right behind them. The flatness of the prairie often made objects appear closer than in reality, so it took them longer to get to Charles' house. After running for three or four minutes the boys slowed to a jog, for their lungs were bursting and their legs were aching. Approaching the burning house with the smoke becoming thicker and thicker, they realized nobody was trying to put out the fire. George, who was by far the fastest runner, sprinted toward the house in time to see a group of men riding off in the distance.

"Charles!" he called as he approached. "Charles, where are you?"

Nobody answered. George stopped for a second, panting so hard he had to lean forward and hold his knees to catch his breath. David quickly came up behind him to catch his breath.

"You see anybody?" David asked in between gasps.

"No," George managed to say. "Nobody."

"Abe, Abe!" the two fathers called as they slowly approached the house.

"Abe!" George's dad called again. "Are you there?"

"Help!" a voice called from in the cabin. "Help, we're in here!"

Sean looked at John who looked back at Sean. What could they do? The house was burning out of control. Flames leaped from every wall and the door was completely ablaze. Smoke billowed out of the holes in the roof so fast and spread through the air making it hard to see and even harder to breathe.

"George, David!" Sean called as he coughed and hacked through the smoke. "Go to the well and get some water. John, you see whether there is another way in. I'll grab a shovel and try to cover the fire with dirt."

Everyone scattered to try to extinguish the fire. The cries from inside the house were getting fainter and fainter. Within minutes all that could be heard was faint coughing.

"It's not working, John!" Sean called. "It's completely out of control!"

"We've got to do something, Dad!" George called. "Charles and Abe are in there, I know it. We can't let them be burned alive, we can't!"

Suddenly, Sean ran to a window, smashed it with his elbow, and jumped back as the flames shot outward.

"Give me those buckets," he said to the boys. "John, give me your shirt."

"What are you doing?" John said in a confused voice taking off his shirt and handing it to Sean.

"I'm making myself a protective cover," Sean said as he dipped John's shirt in the bucket of water and poured the other bucket over his head.

"This should keep me from burning right away," he said as he put John's drenched shirt over his shoulders. "Wish me luck."

"Wait, Dad, you can't," George called but it was too late. With a quick look back at his son and giving him a smile, Sean headed to the broken window.

"Don't worry, son," he said smiling. "I'll be fine."

Without another word, Sean disappeared leaping through the window into the flames.

He landed feet first, then rolled a little until he came to a stop. Immediately, his eyes started to burn and his throat became parched. The sparks from the flames jumped all over him threatening to ignite his clothes any minute.

"Charles! Abe!" he called in between coughs. "Are you there?"

Waving his hands in front of his eyes in an attempt to see better did not help. The smoke completely blinded him; his eyes, now closed, continued to burn and to water. Wrapping John's shirt over his head, he stumbled around the room trying to get his bearings, knowing he could not last much longer, yet refusing to give up.

"What's taking him so long?" George wondered. "Shouldn't he have found them by now?"

"He just went in there," David replied. "Give him a chance."

"Stop standing around, boys," David's father said. "Let's see what we can do about putting out this fire in case Sean can't get out. Quick, go grab some water!"

The boys returned with water as John continued to add dirt to the fire. He was concentrating on the door in case Sean could not come out the same way he entered the house. It seemed to be working a little, and after David and George added their buckets of water he hoped that they might be able to enter the house.

"Oh, my God, Dad," David said suddenly, pointing to the top of the house. "Look!"

John looked up to see the roof beginning to sag under its own weight. Within minutes the blazing logs would come crashing down into the house.

"Sean, you've got to get out of there!" he yelled. "Sean, do you hear me? Sean!"

Inside, Sean was beginning to lose hope. He had managed to move around the room without finding Charles or Abe.

"Charles," he called one more time. "Abe! Charl....ooofff!" He stumbled falling onto the floor.

"Huh?" he heard a small voice say. "Is someone there?"

Realizing he had tripped over Charles, Sean quickly took the shirt off of his head and wrapped it around him.

"Charles, it's me, George's father. Are you alright?"

"I...I don't know," he answered slowly. "Where's my dad?"

Looking down on the floor, Sean could see a little better now and it only took him a moment to see Abe lying a few feet away from Charles.

"He's right over here," Sean answered.

C-c-creakkk! The roof groaned as it began to sag even more. Sean looked up.

"Charles, we've got to get out of here or we'll be killed!" he shouted over the crackle and pop of the flames. "Can you walk?"

"I...I think so," Charles answered, "but what about my dad?"

"I'll drag him," Sean answered. "Do you know which way is out?"

"No!" Charles said panicking. "I can't see a thing and I don't remember where I fell."

"Well, we'll just have to guess," Sean said grabbing Abe by the legs and beginning to move him. "Get going!"

Moving for a few moments on their hands and knees was getting them nowhere. Suddenly, a light appeared ahead of them through the smoke.

"Sean!" a voice yelled from the other side. "I've cleared you a path. Head towards my voice!"

"That way!" Sean yelled at Charles. Recognizing his brother's voice, he felt a sudden surge of extra energy knowing there was now a clear way out, if only they could make it.

Meanwhile, the others waited anxiously on the other side, continuing to pour water and dirt on the fire and calling repeatedly to Sean.

Creak-k-k! The roof groaned again as logs began to fall all around them.

"Dad!" George yelled. "Hurry!"

George looked at the roof and again at the door and back at the roof. They weren't going to make it.

Suddenly, his father appeared in the doorway.

"Dad," George shouted, "you made it!"

"Cough, cough, cough, heck, heck, heck!" Sean burst out as he collapsed on the grass. "I found them, I found them!"

The back part of the roof groaned one last time before the entire roof collapsed into the house.

Several hours later, after the fire had gradually diminished, the once proud house stood as a smoldering ruin—the roof had caved in, all the windows were blown out, and only two of the four walls remained. Charles had passed out, and Abe, who was alive but badly burned, had fallen asleep.

"Ohhhhhh," Abe finally said as he started to stir. "What happened?"

"That's what we'd like to know," John said as he offered some water to Abe.

"J-J-John?" Abe said, drinking the water down in large gulps. "What are you doing here?"

"We were out hunting when we saw the smoke," John answered.

"Smoke?" Abe repeated. "Smoke? My God...the house!...Charles! Is he okay?"

"He's fine, he's fine," Sean answered, moving to talk to Abe now that he was awake. "I pulled him and you out of the house just in time."

"Sean?" Abe said, obviously still confused. "You're here too?"

"He sure is," David answered. Everyone was sitting around Abe now. "And if it wasn't for him, you wouldn't be here at all."

"Huh, what do you mean?" Abe said sitting up in the grass. "My house!"

Abe looked at the smoldering ruins of his house as smoke still rose lightly into the sky from the remains of the walls.

"What have they done to my house?" he cried.

"They?" John repeated. "Who are they?"

"The Missourians," Abe cried. "They stopped by a few minutes ago."

"What would the Missourians want with you?" Sean asked.

"I don't know, I don't know," Abe cried. "They showed up in a foul mood. I was inside the house working when Charles called to me that he saw some men approaching on horseback."

"Yeah," Charles added. "They were riding real fast, but they did not look like they were going anywhere in particular."

"How do you know that?" Sean asked.

"Because they weren't really riding over here," he answered. "They were heading away from the house until one of them noticed us. When he turned his horse in our direction, the others followed and that's when I ran to get Pa."

"What did they want?" George asked.

"I still don't know," Charles answered. "They were real angry. Asked us if we knew anyone in Lawrence and if we ever been to Fort Scott or Missouri."

"What did you say?" David asked, wondering whether Charles had talked about his parents' cause.

"We said of course we knew people in Lawrence, but we didn't mention any names," Abe answered. "We knew that they were looking for abolitionists, so we kept our mouths shut tight."

"But, Dad," Charles interrupted, "I thought they were gonna leave us alone when you explained we were from Illinois and all."

"Me too, son," his father replied. "They all turned to leave when one of them stopped."

"Why did he stop?" John asked. He was beginning to feel guilty that somehow these men were looking for him or at least other abolitionists like him and that Abe had simply been in the way.

"I don't know," Abe answered. "He saw something... something on my table. What was it?"

"My Lord, now I remember," Abe exclaimed. "He saw the book that Regina had loaned me."

"What book?" John asked angrily.

"*Uncle Tom's Cabin*," Abe answered. "*Uncle Tom's Cabin*...you know, the one about the slave's life and all. The one that the Southerners all hate."

"Course I know it," John answered. "I read it three times."

"Hmmpphh," Abe said. "Well, I had just started it. Anyway, these men got angry all of a sudden. Said I musta been one of them abolitionists. I tried to deny it, but they would hear none of it. Next thing I know, one of 'em's grabbing Charles and yelling about burning our house."

"Then what happened?" George asked quickly.

"I don't know much else," Abe said. "Someone knocked me in the back and the next thing I remember was you waking me up."

"I know what happened, Pa," Charles continued. "Someone hit you with the end of their gun; then they threw me next to you. The leader, or whoever he was, pointed his gun at me and told me not to move while the others started the fire. Then, he waited till the last minute to jump out the door and I couldn't do nothing to help you. Lord, Pa, I thought we were gonna die."

"Hey, hey, we ain't dead," Abe quickly said trying to comfort his son. "And we ain't gonna let these ruffians get the best of us, are we, son?"

"No way," Charles answered.

"That's the spirit," Abe said, standing up and looking around the claim.

"But Dad," George suddenly said, "what about them Missourians? Shouldn't we get the sheriff."

"Won't do no good, George," John answered for his brother. "By the time we get the sheriff and he heads out, those men will be long gone and probably back in Missouri."

"But...but," George stuttered.

"Sorry, George," his Uncle John went on. "But this is what life in the K.T. is all about. There's no stopping it and it's only gonna get worse. These pro-slavery men only understand violence. Until the government decides to come in and do something about this we're gonna have to handle them ourselves."

"Handling them ourselves is what got us into this mess in the first place," Sean snapped at his brother. He knew all about John's raid into Missouri to attack slaveholders. There was a good chance that Abe's house was burnt by those very people who John had attacked.

"Well maybe," John said, knowing his brother was trying to partially blame him for this disaster on him. John wasn't about to let him start an argument in front of Abe and Charles, especially while their house smoldered in the background. "But that don't matter now. Soon enough this will all be settled and out of our hands. For now, let's try to help Abe with his house."

Everyone looked curiously at John. What did he mean this would all be settled soon enough? It was getting worse not better and the government certainly wasn't doing anything about it. Did he know something they did not? Was something about to happen here in Lawrence? Was he going on another raid? David hoped that his father was just talking and was not about to leave him again. He finally had managed to open up to his father and they were getting along great.

"Please, don't spoil it all now," David thought to himself as he picked up some burnt wood and threw it in the pile the others had started. "Please, just stay here and don't worry about these problems. I want to be with you, Dad."

Chapter 12
The Secret Plan

George quietly entered the house. He knew that David was inside looking after Aunt Regina and he didn't want to disturb them.

"How is she?" George asked David.

"The same," David said softly. His voice was etched with worry and despair. His mother had fallen sick again and this time it was even worse. Ever since they had returned from the hunting trip with news of the Bishop's house being destroyed, Regina felt on edge. She was uptight, angry, and then suddenly quiet for days at a time. No one had been able to figure out her moods, not even David's father. He appeared more uptight than she.

By June, Regina began to experience fainting spells. One day when David was returning from work he came home to find her unconscious on the floor. She'd been that way for over a month now.

"Think she'll ever wake up?" George asked.

"I don't know," David said shrugging his shoulders. He placed a wet washcloth on her head.

"Is she still hot?"

"Yup," David said.

"When was the last time you talked to the doctor?" George asked.

"Who knows, who cares," David said bitterly. "They don't know anything. All they say is to let her rest and to try a few medicines."

"Yeah, I know," George said. "I don't think I can ever remember a doctor helping somebody."

There was another pause as both boys looked quietly at the bed.

"Your dad still acting strange?" George asked.

"Kind of," David answered. "He keeps mumbling everywhere he goes and he's not playing with me much. He'll pace back and forth in the room, try to talk to Mom, then storm out of the house, and not return for hours."

"What, do you think, has gotten into him?"

"I dunno," David answered. "Maybe he's just worried about mom or some other thing."

"Remember what he said that time at Charles' house after it was burned?" George asked David.

"You mean about it all being over soon?" David said.

"Yeah," George replied. "Maybe that's got something to do with it."

"Maybe," David repeated quietly.

"How is she...how is she?" David's father suddenly cried as he burst into the room. He was waving a letter in the air that had obviously just been opened.

"How is she?" he asked again.

"The same," David answered.

"Damn," his father cursed. "Why did this have to happen now?"

"What happened, Dad?" David asked curiously.

"Has she said anything," his father said, ignoring David's question completely.

"Not a word," David answered quickly.

"Damn," his father cursed again as he stormed out of the house.

"What was that all about," George asked David.

"Beats me," David replied. "I've never been able to figure him out."

As the days dragged into summer David's father had become more and more upset pacing constantly and even talking to himself. Meanwhile, George and his father were trying to make plans to settle elsewhere as soon as Regina recovered from her illness. Kansas was too crazy for them, and they didn't like living in the shadow of David's dad and his weird habits. They had already decided to stay away from Boston since that would only put them under the control of George's Uncle Robert. On their own, in a new city, Sean and George could be father and son with no one to bother them or to tell them what to do.

By August, George hoped that they might be able to leave soon since Regina had recovered enough to talk and sit up. Unfortunately, she clearly was still very sick. Occasionally, she talked nonsense about faraway places and monsters and demons. Other times she was perfectly normal, discussing the weather, local politics, or even the upcoming presidential elections. One day when David, George, and his father were returning home from a quick game of catch, everything changed.

"Where's John?" George's father said as he walked into the house. "It was his turn to be watching Regina."

"I don't see him anywhere, Dad," George said.

"Guys, over here!" David called to them.

Sean and George ran to the bed where Regina lay. Her eyes were wide open, and she was shaking her head vigorously.

"No! No!" she was crying repeatedly.

"No what, Mother?" David cried in an attempt to get her to explain.

"No! No!" she called again.

"Regina, sister," Sean said suddenly, grabbing Regina by the shoulders, holding her tight and staring into her eyes. "It's me, Sean. What's the matter?"

"Sean?" Regina asked, straightening up and looking firmly at him. "Sean, is that you?"

"Yes, honey, it's me," he said gently. "What's wrong? Where's John?"

"John? John?" she repeated. "Oh my God, you have to stop him! He'll be killed."

"Stop him?" Sean said. "Stop him from what? You've got to slow down and explain, dear."

"He's gone off," Regina answered quickly, trying to calm down and speak in a normal voice. "He said he's got to join Brown before it's too late."

"John Brown?" Sean asked.

"Yes...yes, of course," she said with a little irritation. "Of course John Brown. He's got some plan to free the slaves in Harpers Ferry, Virginia, and start some kind of war!"

"What?" Sean said. "I knew that John was involved with Brown, yet I never thought he'd do something like this."

"You must be mistaken, Mother," David interrupted. "Dad wouldn't do something so illegal."

"I'm not mistaken, young man," his mother answered sternly. "I may have been sick for awhile, but I know what your father has told me."

"But maybe it's not as serious as it sounds," David said desperately. "Maybe it's only another raid."

"No, it's serious," his mother replied quickly. "Would your father have kissed me good-bye as if it were forever if he were not doubting his return?"

"But why now?" Sean asked.

"I'm not sure," Regina answered. "I do know that whatever Brown's got planned it's going to be soon. John said that he stayed here as long as he could waiting for me to recover but that it was 'now or never' as he put it."

"That's why he was acting so crazy," George said. "He was waiting to leave until you got better."

"That's right," Sean said. "And it must be happening real soon. He would never have run out of here with Regina still sick."

"Are we gonna go after him, Pa?" George asked.

"You have to!" Regina broke in. "You have to! If you don't he'll die and maybe he'll have started something terrible as well!"

"How will we find him?" Sean asked.

"Just follow the roads to Harpers Ferry!" Regina said quickly.

"That's over two hundred miles!" Sean argued. "How will we ever find him or catch him?"

"Take the picture with you," Regina said slowly and calmly. The strength in her voice was beginning to return as she was forced to help with details. "The one he had made special for me at Christmas. Ask around at all the inns. There are only a few places to stay along the way, and with all his bags he won't be moving as fast, so you should go soon."

"What bags?"

"He's taking extra rifles and supplies," Regina answered impatiently. "Didn't you notice them piled up in the back."

"All those nice, new Sharp's rifles?" David exclaimed. "He told me that he was holding them for the sheriff."

"Well, he wasn't," Regina said. "Now, you've got to get going. Please!"

"But we can't leave you alone," George said.

"I'll stay," David replied. He was too worried about his mother to leave her alone or with a stranger. Besides, he thought, if his dad was involved illegally in something, he didn't want to see it. "You guys get my dad and bring him back safely, O.K.?"

George and his father looked at each other shrugging their shoulders. What choice did they have? They couldn't let John go and get himself killed, and if they stayed Regina would work herself up into such a fury that she would get even sicker.

"Well, Dad," George said with the hint of a smile on his face. "It looks as if we're going on yet another chase of an Adams' family member."

"I guess so," his father said seriously. "Only this time if we don't find him quickly, it could mean his life."

It took almost all morning to ready the horses. George suggested they travel the new train since it would be so much faster. Unfortunately, his father had told him that the trains were unpredictable. Besides, they needed to try to follow the same path that John may have taken. They knew that he had taken a horse, if for no other reason than to give him a certain level of freedom and to carry the extra weapons. With few main roads to Harpers Ferry and with some luck they would be able to catch him at one of the inns along the way.

By the time they were ready to leave, Regina had fallen into a deep sleep, so David had come outside to see them off.

"Good-bye David," George said, once the horses had been packed. It was getting close to noon and they needed to go if they were to make any distance at all today. "Take good care of your mother."

"I will," David said sadly. "And you take good care of yourselves."

"We will," Sean answered. "And don't worry, we'll find your father."

"Just don't let him do anything stupid," David said, trying to sound brave.

"Don't worry," his Uncle Sean repeated. "Everything will be fine. You take care of my beautiful sister-in-law."

"C'mon, Dad, we gotta go," George interrupted.

"Yeah, get going," David added. "I hate long good-byes anyway."

"Bye," they both called as they turned the horses away from the house.

David watched his uncle and cousin ride off. He was alone now. Charles would have no time to stop by to see them with their house being so badly burnt and needing so much work before winter returned. Who would David talk to? Who would he play with?

Suddenly, an idea hit him. He ran into the house and returned as quickly as he could.

"Hey, George!" he yelled running after them. "George!"

George stopped his horse and looked back.

"Catch!" David called as he threw the baseball in George's direction.

"What's this for?" George called back as he caught the ball with two hands.

"It's for good luck!" David yelled back. "I won't be needing it, and you and your Dad will need something to do when you're not chasing my old man."

"Thanks, David," Uncle Sean yelled back. "Take care."

As David stood and watched the figures slowly disappear into the prairie, he suddenly realized the loneliness in his life now. In the past there always had been someone who had slept in his room, who had talked and laughed with him, and who even had enjoyed a fight with him. Now, there was no one. His mother was barely able to speak and when she did it hardly made any sense. What would he do to ease his loneliness.

"Please...please come back," David cried to himself as his uncle and cousin finally disappeared from sight.

Chapter 13
On the Road Again

George was bored. This trip was nothing like the first one with his father. This time, there was no exitement, no feelings of new lands and adventures waiting, only mile after mile of endless road with nothing to look at and nothing to do. George and his father rarely talked and when they did it was usually about where they would stop and what they would eat. The roads, although busy with travelers, were not as noisy and crazy as the first time. It was now October and many of the anxious settlers on the roads rushed to avoid the onset of winter.

The traveling was even slower than George thought it would be, for they stopped at every inn and tavern, inquiring about Uncle John. Nearing Virginia they feared he would arrive ahead of them. By the second week of October, George and his father were getting so desperate to find Uncle John that they slept only a few hours each night, ate a rushed breakfast, and rode as hard as they could from town to town. Luckily, at a tavern outside of Cumberland, Maryland, a local bartender said that he had talked to a man a few hours earlier, who sounded and looked like George's Uncle

John. The bartender had directed the man to an inn approximately 15 miles down the road. If George and his father hurried they might catch him before dark!

George's father downed his beer, threw a quarter at the bartender, and rushed out of the tavern.

"C'mon, George, c'mon!" he yelled.

"I'm coming, I'm coming," George yelled, rubbing his back with his right hand. "I need a rest for a second that's all."

"We can't, son," Sean said sternly. "This could be our last chance to catch your uncle before he goes to wherever Brown is hiding."

"Hiding?" George repeated.

"Of course," his dad answered quickly. "Do you think Brown is going to stand in the middle of the street to announce his plans. He's got to be hiding somewhere awaiting his other friends like your uncle. Now c'mon!"

They rode as fast as they could. Occasionally George's dad had to slow down because of George's smaller horse. Within an hour they sighted the inn, which the bartender had described.

"Set the horses in the stable," his father said. "I'll go inside to ask whether John has been here."

George tied the horses up, grabbed the gear, and headed inside where his father was waiting.

"He's here alright," his dad said.

"Where?" George asked excitedly, looking around the small room with a desk and bench set aside for travelers.

"He's in there having a drink," his dad said, pointing to an adjoining room. "He arrived a few hours ago."

"Great!" George cried, running towards the room. "Let's go!"

"Not so fast, son," his father interrupted him, putting his arm in front of George's chest to stop his movement. "We've got to do this carefully. Your uncle is very uptight about all this and there's no telling what he will do when we find him. You keep quiet for awhile until I've got him figured out. O.K.?"

"Sure, Dad, sure," George assured him. "I'll be good."

"Good, let's go then," his father said as he walked into the room.

Uncle John was sitting in the corner with his back to them, staring out the window in deep thought, nursing a beer, and playing with the small steak left on his plate.

"Hello, John," Sean said softly as he walked to the table. "Fancy seeing you here."

"Huh?" John said turning around. "Sean?"

"Hi," George added. He couldn't resist smiling at the look of shock on his uncle's face.

"George?" he gasped, spitting his beer out and setting the glass down hard on the table. "What are you two doing here?"

"Can we sit down?" Sean said, ignoring the question and pulling out a chair for himself.

"Of course, of course," his brother mumbled.

George and his father pulled up a chair to the table and sat down gently. John was obviously nervous as his shaking hand pulled the beer glass up to his lips and he gulped another sip of his beer.

"A couple of beers over here," Sean called to the bartender as he waved in his direction. "And something to eat to. Whatcha in the mood for, son?"

"How about some steak like Uncle John's eating?" George asked.

"Sounds good," his father said as he again turned toward the bartender. "And a couple of steaks too, please."

"Coming up!" the bartender yelled to them.

John remained silent as he took another gulp of beer.

"So, John," Sean began as the bartender placed the beers on the table, "what takes you so far from home?"

"You must be thinking I am a terrible husband," John began nervously. "But I assure you that what I am doing has to be done."

"Just what are you doing?" Sean asked slowly. He was surprised at his brother's willingness to talk, for he had always been so secretive in the past. Now, he was opening up awful quickly. Maybe it was because they caught him by surprise.

"Something that will forever change this country and save us all in the eyes of the Lord," John answered.

Sean looked at him curiously while George took a sip of the beer. Thirsty, he quickly drained it without taking a breath.

"George!" his father yelled when George dropped the empty glass on the table.

"Sorry, Dad, I was really thirsty," George answered. "Can I have another?"

"No," his father answered quickly. "You know I never let you have more than one beer. You're just a boy."

"But Dad," George whined. "We've been riding real hard, and I've had to act like a man for this whole trip now. Can't you treat me like a big kid this once, please?"

"Well," his father thought.

"Please," George begged. He knew he was taking advantage of his father. Sean hated to act like a mean guy and get in a fight with his son in front of other people, especially when he was too busy trying to find out what John was up to.

"Alright," his father consented. "Bartender!"

George smiled as his father waved at the bartender and then turned his attention back to his brother.

"I'm sorry, John," Sean continued. "What were you saying?"

"Listen, Sean," John whispered as he leaned across the table. He had had time to think while George and his dad argued. "Why don't you join me?"

"Join you?" Sean said in shock as he leaned back on the chair. This was definitely not the reaction he had expected from his brother.

"Sure," John answered. "You lived in the K.T. You know what it's all about. Besides, you're a good shot and we could use men like you."

"We?" Sean repeated, trying to pretend he knew nothing so John would explain it all.

"You know," John whispered again. "Brown and his men."

Sean nodded and waited.

"He's got this great plan, Sean," John continued. "He's gonna make this land finally safe for all of us by ending slavery once and for all."

John stopped suddenly as the bartender approached the table.

"Here's some more beer for you," he said, placing them on the table. "Your steaks will be out in a minute."

"How's he going to do that?" Sean asked once the bartender had left.

"He's planning a raid on the Federal arsenal at Harpers Ferry," John answered.

"The arsenal?" Sean repeated, trying to stay calm.

"Yeah," John continued. "Brown figures that there are plenty of weapons there to launch a slave rebellion throughout the area."

"What?" Sean gasped. "How will he get the slaves together?"

"He won't need to," John answered. "Once they hear that Brown is organizing a rebellion to give them their freedom the slaves will tear off their bonds, flock to his side, and march through the land setting free more of their fellow slaves and laying waste to the plantations that enslave them. It will be glorious, Sean, glorious!"

Sean sat back in horror. His brother was really crazy—slaves marching through the land, killing whites and attacking towns. Sean did not like slavery but this was no way to end it—death to hundreds of innocent people.

"But what about the army?" George suddenly added, finishing his second beer. He had kept quiet like his dad asked, but now he was beginning to feel light-headed and was having difficulty paying attention.

"Brown says that by the time they get there, the rebellion will be so spread out that they won't be able to stop it," his uncle answered.

"But whash about the innocent white pee-pul who'll be killed?" George managed to say tongue-tied, hoping his dad hadn't noticed.

"There are no innocents, don't you understand that?" John almost shouted. The other people in the room turned their heads and stared at them.

"Quiet down, John," Sean said as he raised his hand to motion John to sit down. Then, he also took another look at George who seemed to be swaying funny in his chair.

"Everyone is guilty," John went on softly. "Everyone who tolerates and accepts this terrible system of slavery."

"I'm not guilty," George said slowly. His head was really beginning to spin now.

"We all are, George," John answered quickly. "Everyone who owns a slave, or does nothing to help a slave, or sits back and watches as his fellow human is treated worse than an animal. We all are guilty."

"Here's your steak," the bartender said as he placed the plates on the table. Suddenly, George did not feel like eating anymore.

"Dad," George said as he sat back and held his stomach. "I'm not hungry anymore."

"What?" his father exclaimed. "I paid good money for that steak, and you haven't eaten all day."

"I'm jush not hungry," George mumbled.

"George Adams!" his father called out. "Are you drunk?"

"No!" George reacted. "Of course not!"

"Listen, John," Sean said quickly knowing that now was the only chance he would get to keep John on his side. "I'm going to have to take care of George, but what you say sounds really interesting. Alright if I ride with you in the morning?"

"Yeah, sure!" John said as his face lit up. "You know you're always welcome with me, little brother!"

"Ohhhh," George groaned as his face fell smack into the mashed potatoes.

"What time are you leaving?" George's dad asked, shaking his head in disgust as he picked George's head up by the back of his neck.

"Dawn," John answered. "Think you can make it?"

"We'll be there," Sean promised as he began to clean George's face with a napkin.

"Bartender," Sean called, pointing to his steak, "I'll take this to my room."

"See ya tomorrow, brother," John called out.

"Sure," Sean said as he left the room with a wave.

"And Sean," John added at the last moment, "I'm proud of you."

Chapter 14
The Fight

"Get up, son, get up," George seemed to hear a voice saying as a hand softly shook him in bed.

"Ohhhhhhh," he moaned, rubbing his eyes with his hand and starting to sit up. "My head."

"Feels like it weighs a hundred pounds, huh, son?" his father said standing over him.

"No, more like two hundred," George replied. "What happened?"

"You passed out," his father answered. "Your face fell smack dab into the potatoes, and I had to clean you up and haul you into bed while your uncle looked on and laughed."

"I'm sorry, Dad," George said as he started to rise.

"No big deal, son," his father said with a chuckle. "I've more than had my share of days like that. I just never should have let you drink beer on an empty stomach after such a long, hard ride."

"Yeah," George agreed as he rubbed his head again and began to get dressed. His stomach felt as if there were little bugs flying around in it, and his forehead pounded with each beat of his heart. If his dad ever let him have two beers again he swore he would never drink them.

The first signs of sunlight shone in their dark room, so they knew to get ready quickly. Sean wanted to avoid any chance of John leaving without them, so he wanted to be down at the horses' station before sunup.

The cool night air made George feel much better. Taking a deep breath he felt the crisp, tingly sensation of the early morning dew tickling his nose. A few birds chirped in the distance, and the crickets were so loud that George could barely hear his boots scraping the dirt as he walked along. Behind him the first rays of sunlight were streaking over the horizon. Fireflies were still buzzing and shining their little lights on and off in the last moments of darkness.

"Good morning, Emerald," George said to his horse as he stroked her soft mane with his hands. He had grown quite fond of his horse ever since he had ridden her out of the stables of Boston. She had a soft brown coat and a beautiful black mane that whipped in the breeze when she ran. George had named her Emerald because her bright green eyes reminded him of the stories of Ireland that his Aunt Patricia had always told. "The Emerald Island," she had called it, and George would often imagine riding his horse through the beautiful green countryside where his family had come from.

"She ready to ride?" his father asked George as he too was stroking the mane of his horse.

"Soon as I strap these bags to her and give her some breakfast," George replied. "Where are we going?"

"I don't know," his dad answered as he handed a bucket of oats to George. "We're going wherever your uncle wants us to go."

"Huh," George frowned as he grabbed the bucket and put it under Emerald's mouth so she could eat. "I thought the plan was to stop him."

"It is," his father answered. "But I want to try to stop him without using force. I'm hoping that if I pretend to be on his side, I can eventually convince him to change his mind or at least delay him enough until it's all over."

"How you gonna do that?" George asked.

"I'm not sure," he replied. "I've got to make him think that I really feel the way he does and at the same time try to—"

"Good morning," John waved as he suddenly approached. "How did you boys sleep."

"Fine," they answered nervously. George worried that his uncle overheard their conversation.

"How's your head, George," Uncle John said with a laugh.

"Sore," George said slowly, upset at his uncle for reminding him about the pain.

"Well, it won't be the first time, if you're anything like your dad, that is," John laughed, smiling at his brother and patting him on the back.

"So, John, where are we off to?" he said.

"You still interested?" John said cautiously. It seemed that he was having second thoughts about inviting them along.

"Yeah, sure," Sean answered quickly. "I didn't ride all the way from Kansas just to turn around."

"You might have if you were trying to stop me," John returned in an unfriendly tone.

"H-hey," Sean answered nervously. "If I was trying to stop you, wouldn't I have done it already?"

"Maybe," his brother answered. "But just the same I think I'll wait to tell you where we're going until we get there."

"Sure, fine," Sean replied, giving a nervous look at George. "Whatever you say."

They rode in silence for several hours. John was definitely anxious about bringing his brother along, especially when it included his son, George. John had suggested that they leave George behind, but Sean would hear none of it. The two men argued back and forth about it until John finally realized that his nephew could wait at John Brown's farm while the men went on their raid.

Sean had tried to find out where the farm was but again John became suspicious and angry, so Sean had to drop it. By the time afternoon arrived, George was beginning to think that they would never be able to stop his uncle unless they shot him.

"Dad, you've got to do something. We're less than a hard days' ride from Harpers Ferry," George whispered at a resting point along the way. His uncle had disappeared into the bushes to go to the bathroom so this was one of the few moments they had alone.

"I know, I know," his father whispered back. "But he hasn't given me any chance to talk at all."

"Can't you tell him that breaking the law is wrong?" George asked.

"What? and have him run off and leave us in the dust," his father replied. "Your uncle has been breaking the law in the Kansas Territory for years. Heck, even when he lived in Boston he broke the law to hide runaway slaves."

"Yeah, but this is different. This is war," George said.

"Don't you think I know that? But what am I supposed to do? Shoot my own brother?" his father asked.

"Ahhh, that felt great," John announced as he came out of the bushes. "Are you sure you boys don't have to go?"

"No thanks," Sean said.

"I gotta go, so I could be a while." George winked at his dad.

"Well, hurry up," his uncle said impatiently. "We gotta hit the road."

"Talk to him now. Maybe you can talk better with me outta here," George whispered to his dad.

His father smiled at George, patted him on the back and said, "Don't rush it too much, son. I don't want to have to stop again."

"Kids," John said shaking his head and approaching his brother. "Sometimes I don't know whether to love 'em or to hate 'em."

"I know what you mean. Sometimes I wanna wring George's neck and other times I want to hug him," Sean said.

"Hmmmpphhh," John mumbled, sitting down on the side of the road and playing with a small wildflower.

"You miss David and Thomas and your girls?" Sean asked as he joined John on the side of the road. He was hoping to get John talking about his family. Maybe, if he could get John to think about them, he might reconsider his plan.

"You bet I do," John replied. "I haven't seen Thomas and the girls in years. Lord, if they've grown as much as David, then I won't recognize them."

"They have grown, especially Helen. When you left, she was four years old?" Sean said.

"Yeah," John mumbled. "She used to sit on my lap and squeeze my neck so hard I could barely breathe. I would stand up and she would still be dangling, holding my neck, kicking her legs, and giggling up a storm."

"Yeah, I remember that," Sean said. "We certainly had some good times in that house."

"And some bad," John added.

"What will happen to them if we don't succeed?" Sean asked, trying to keep John thinking about his kids.

"I don't know," John said slowly. "I suppose they'll live with Robert."

"All our kids with our older brother, Robert?" Sean said doubtfully. "Boy that would be a sight to see."

"I suppose so," John said, hanging his head and staring between his legs at the ground.

"He probably will tell them all kinds of awful stories about us knowing how he feels about you," Sean quickly added. He could feel like he was getting somewhere in the conversation.

"What do you mean 'how he feels about me'?" John asked, lifting his head.

"Ever since you and Regina left, Robert has said nothing but awful things about you and your ideas," Sean answered with just a little exaggeration. Their older brother did not like John and Regina leaving their kids in Boston and he took every opportunity to let the family know that.

"He's called you abolitionist hotheads," Sean continued quickly. "He's made fun of your ideas by teaching the children that people like you and Regina are ruining our country."

"What?" John said angrily, standing up and beginning to pace. "How dare he teach my children such things?"

"He's even tried to remove them from school," Sean continued, hoping to get John really angry. "But fortunately, I've managed to stop him. Of course, now with me gone—"

"That son of a ———," John swore.

"Maybe if we didn't join Brown right away," Sean decided to take his chance now.

"What do you mean, not join Brown right away?" John asked abruptly, turning suddenly to face his brother.

"I...I mean," Sean said nervously, "maybe we can try to straighten things out with your children first and then join Brown."

"We can't do that," John sharply replied. "There's no time. Brown may be launching his raid right now. If we turn around here, we will never be able to help."

"But," Sean said slowly, knowing he was beginning to lose the argument but persisted. "Aren't your children important to you?"

"Of course they are," John yelled suddenly, his face beginning to turn red and his arms flying in the air. "But this is war, I tell you, war. Not the obvious kind with armies and cannon, but a war against slavery and oppression that John Brown is finally going to win."

"But how, John?" Sean pleaded. "How can a small band of men like ourselves hope to overthrow the United States Government?"

"We're not overthrowing the whole government," John shouted. "We are liberating the slaves under the control of that government."

"But it's wrong," Sean finally said, expressing words from the bottom of his heart.

"What?" his brother cried, stopping in his tracks and staring at Sean.

"We can't take the law into our own hands, John," Sean said slowly and quietly.

"We have to!" John argued. "We have to! Whenever a law is one-sided it is the responsibility of the people to countermand the law. This is no different than our revolution 80 years ago when George Washington fought for the freedom of his fellow Americans against an unjust British king. We, too, are fighting to free our fellow human beings from the evil government that protects these slaveholders."

"But hundreds, maybe thousands, will be killed," Sean pleaded.

"'An eye for an eye,' as it says in the Bible, Sean," John answered coldly. "These slaveholders have been destroying the lives of thousands of blacks since the first days of our country. The owners make money while the people get nothing for all their hard work, toil, and sweat. If they don't do the work, he beats them. He can even sell them to other slaveowners or split up families to make a profit! To him, these people are nothing more than property, like the sofa in the living room! Well, it's time to put an end to it!"

"Please, John," Sean begged.

"Please, what?" John challenged. "Are you saying you want out?"

"I'm saying I want you out," Sean replied, quickly adding, "Regina wants you out. David wants you out. They sent me to stop you. Please, for their sake if for no one else's, stop what you are doing!"

John stopped and thought for a moment.

"No!" he said angrily. "I can't stop for anyone, not even them. What I'm doing must be done and nothing can stop me, not even you!"

Suddenly, John jumped on his horse and turned away.

"Wait, John," Sean yelled at him, "I can't let you go."

Ignoring his brother's plea, John turned his horse onto the road. Instantly, Sean jumped on his horse and gave chase.

George ran out of the bushes where he was watching.

"Wait, Dad, wait!" he yelled.

George looked around. There was no one around to help him. He looked ahead again at his father and uncle, who by now were already turning the corner and racing down the road. George jumped on his horse to follow them.

"Stop, John, please," Sean yelled again as his horse slowly began to catch up to John's. "You've got to listen to me!"

"I'll listen no more," John shouted back as he whipped the reins of his horse again to speed it up.

Sean couldn't let this chase continue much longer. He looked down the road that was narrowing as they climbed higher and higher through the Appalachian Mountains. Over the edge, Sean could see the sudden drop to the cliffs and rocks below. Whipping the horse's reins one more time, Sean's horse, not weighed down with as much equipment as his brother's, gained on John and came up beside him. Sean then loosened his feet out of his saddle and climbed onto the back of his horse.

"What are you doing?" John said suddenly, turning to see his brother right next to him.

"Raaaarrr!" Sean yelled as he jumped off his horse and grabbed the mane of John's. The impact knocked both of them violently off the horse and onto the ground.

"You crazy fool!" John yelled at his brother as he struggled to get up.

"You made me do it!" Sean yelled back, turning towards his brother.

"Arrgghh," Sean screamed as he tried to stand, his leg all twisted from the fall. It felt like a hot knife had suddenly been thrown into it. Trying to slowly stand he backed away from John.

"I'm not going to let you stop me," John warned as he started towards his limping brother.

Sean backed away. Looking up the road, the horses had already disappeared around the bend. He looked back to see George coming into view. He steadied himself for the fight about to happen.

John threw a punch at his brother. Sean deflected it, but he stumbled again on his bad leg. John noticed this and suddenly turned away.

"What was he doing?" Sean thought.

John headed towards the edge of the road where the rocks suddenly gave way to a huge cliff. At first, Sean thought his brother was going to jump, but then John turned around again holding a dead tree branch in his hand.

Sean held up his hands.

"Now wait, John," Sean pleaded. "You've already lost. Your horse, rifles, and supplies are gone and there's no way you can make it to Harpers Ferry on time now."

"Raaaarr," John screamed as he swung the branch at Sean's bad leg.

"Aaahhhh," Sean cried. As he crumpled to the ground, his bones cracked under the pounding of the branch. "Stop, stop!" he begged.

"Dad!" George suddenly yelled as he approached the men and dismounted from his horse. "Dad!"

"Stay back, George," his father called as he slowly rose to his feet. Sean's pain in his leg was intense. His vision suddenly blurred, yet he managed to stand again to face his brother. "This is between John and me."

"Fine with me," John said, looking squarely into his brother's eyes, dropping the branch and raising his fists.

Sean did the same, and within seconds the two men exchanged blows. At first, they were only able to block and dodge. Eventually, the pain in Sean's bum leg weakened him, letting John get through with his punches.

John punched Sean twice in the face and once in the stomach. Sean let out a huge gasp of air. When he bent down for an instant John used that opportunity to get his fist underneath him hitting Sean squarely on the chin. Sean stumbled back and almost fell. He could tell that he was losing the fight.

With his last bit of strength and ignoring the pain in his leg, Sean ran at his brother full force. The action caught John by surprise and the two men fell to the ground near the cliff as they rolled around trying to get an advantage.

Meanwhile, George was panicking. All he could do was watch while his father and uncle tried to kill each other. He looked everywhere hoping for some sudden idea. When the two men fell to the ground near the cliff, George feared that they would both tumble over and be gone forever. Then, he remembered his dad's fight with the stranger. Reaching into his pocket, he pulled out the baseball that David had thrown to him for good luck. The men were so close together though that he still could do nothing. He waited and aimed, waited again, and aimed. It seemed like hours.

When John suddenly sat on top of his father to get a good position to finish him off, George reacted instantly. The ball sailed through the air hitting his uncle in the forehead.

"Aaahhh," he cried falling backwards and grabbing his head.

Sean scrambled out from underneath his brother in an effort to escape.

"Aaaahh," John continued as his left hand wiped the blood off his forehead.

Then George noticed his uncle's right hand reaching for his gun. He aimed it at Sean.

"Dad, watch out!" George screamed.

The sudden scream caught John by surprise. He spun around with his gun aimed towards George. Unfortunately, the quick motion loosened some rocks at his feet causing him to stumble backwards.

"John, John!" Sean cried. "Lookout!"

But it was too late. John unfortunately lost his footing and fell off the cliff.

"Aaaaahhhhhhhhhh!" George heard his uncle scream and scream and scream as the voice slowly trailed off into the valley below.

George turned, looking in horror at his father. Uncle John was dead.

John Brown

The Tragic Prelude, a mural of John Brown, by John Steuart Curry, circa 1937–42, National Archives

Chapter 15
John Brown

George was lost and he couldn't understand why. His father had told him to follow the road in a general direction to arrive at Harpers Ferry, but it was getting close to midnight and he still saw no sign of the town.

"If only Dad were here, he would know what to do," George thought. His dad had insisted that he stay on the road in camp while George sought help.

"You've got to warn the townspeople, George," his father had said once the shock of John's death had left him. "You've got to ride as fast as you can before it's too late."

"M...me?" George stuttered.

"Yes, you," his father said softly as he pulled George to his side, held him close, and looked him straight in the eye.

"You're the only one who can save all those lives in the town," his father continued. "I can't go. My leg won't let me ride and you can't bring me along."

"But I can't leave you here alone," George cried desperately. The thought of riding alone to some strange place terrified him, especially after watching his uncle fall hundreds of feet to his death.

"I'll be fine," George's dad went on. "I can use all the provisions you have sitting on Emerald's back to keep me well fed and warm. Even if I have to sit here for several days, someone's sure to be traveling by real soon. And if that doesn't happen, you can send help for me after you get there. It's only a few more hours' ride."

"B-but, but," George tried to argue.

"No buts, George. You've got to do it. Those people in Harpers Ferry have no idea what John Brown is planning. If you don't warn them, not only could hundreds of people die but a war might even start that could destroy the whole country."

"But what will I tell them?"

"Just tell them what your uncle had planned," George's father said comfortingly. "You know the whole story. You're a smart boy. You can handle it."

"Oh, okay," George agreed. His father's confidence in him made him feel a little better and he was right. There was no other choice.

"Now, hurry up and get going," his father urged him. "The sun will be setting soon and you're still several hours away even at a full pace."

They hugged. It was a strong, soft hug, the kind you give to someone when you leave forever. George did not want to let go, but he had to. With a quick good-bye and a wave of his hand, George rode off towards Harpers Ferry to find John Brown. Turning one last time to look back at his dad, he couldn't help but wonder whether he would ever see him again.

That was more than seven hours ago. George still had not reached the town and he wasn't even sure that he was traveling in the right direction. After dark he had begun to lose his bearings even though the moonlight shone bright enough to ride at a slow trot. Once or twice he may have turned the wrong way, he thought nervously. What if he never made it?

"Hold it right there!" a voice suddenly shouted from the darkness.

George turned to see a man walk out of the bushes towards him. He was wearing a long, gray overcoat and carrying a Sharp rifle in his left hand.

"What are you doing out here this late at night?" the man said in an angry tone.

"Uh...I was just...I was just—"

"Never mind!" the man said angrily, pointing his gun at George and motioning towards the ground. "Get off your horse!"

Without another word George slowly slid down off his horse and stood where the man had pointed. His angry voice indicated a hint of panic in it, and George could tell that if he didn't do exactly what the man said, he would not hesitate to shoot him immediately.

"This way!" the man said, pointing the gun down the road in the direction George had been going.

Within minutes they had left behind George's horse and were walking alone on the dark road. The noises of the crickets, frogs, owls, and even the occasional wolf cry rang through the night. George began to panic in the eerie, dark mist wondering who this man was and what was he going to do with him. Had the raid started already?

George turned suddenly at the sound of horses and carriages coming down the road. The man with the gun held up his hand motioning the driver to stop the carriage for a minute.

"I found this kid riding down the road," he said to another man who also was dressed in a gray overcoat and carrying a Sharp rifle.

"What's he doing here?" the other man said.

"I don't know," he replied. "The kid was too nervous to answer."

"Well, throw him in the wagon with the others."

"You heard him, kid. Get moving."

As George walked to where the man was pointing, he saw an old wagon being pulled by four horses. Reaching the back of it, George could see men sitting in it. One man was white and the others were black. All but three of them were wearing the same gray overcoats and carrying rifles.

"Get in," the man said.

Climbing into the wagon, George was forced to sit next to the three unarmed black men. With a sudden lurch, the wagon moved forward into the darkness.

"What you be doin' here?" said the man sitting next to George.

"Ummm," George mumbled. He had no idea who these people were, whether they were friends or foe, and what they were going to do with him.

"It be alright," the man continued. "I be captured too."

"Captured?" George repeated.

"Dat's right. Dose men break into me master's house and tell him to come along wit dem. Den dey tell me that we are gonna be free and dat we need to help them free others."

"Oh, my God," George gasped. "It has started."

"What has started?" the man asked.

"Quiet, boy," one of the armed men suddenly interrupted, pointing his gun towards George and giving him a cold stare.

George immediately shut his mouth while his mind began to race. He was too late! The raid had begun. Where were they headed and where was John Brown? Had the town already been taken? What were they going to do with him?

The wagon stopped again. The man who had first caught George appeared at the back and motioned them to get out.

"You," he said to the freed slave next to George, "take this and watch the boy."

The man handed the slave a long, sharp pike before he ran off to join the others. The freed slave then turned around to face George.

"Sit," he said nervously, pointing the pike at George.

Loud bangs and crashes shattered the quiet night. Shouting from the raiders and screams of women added to the confusion. George could not see anything except shadows.

"Murder! Murder!" women screamed.

"My God," George thought. "What is going on?"

Within seconds the raiders returned with more prisoners. An older man and his son were shoved into the wagon as well as four more freed slaves.

"What is the meaning of this?" the older man shouted. "I demand to see your leader."

"You aren't in a position to demand anything," one of the raiders said as he pushed the man back. "You have been taken prisoner by the Provisional Army of the United States."

"Army...what army?" the man shouted back. "All I see are a few outlaws dressed in gray."

"We are only a small part of a larger force that will liberate all the slaves in Virginia and put an end to your hated way of life."

"You're crazy," the man's son said.

"Maybe," the raider said slowly. "But you are our prisoners and you are at our mercy to do with as we please. Now, I suggest that you sit down and be quiet before I lose my patience."

The man fell backwards into the wagon where he remained for the duration of the ride. His son sat next to George, both of them prohibited to speak. As the wagon continued down the road, George looked for a way to escape or to do something to stop the raiders, but he felt helpless. With at least three- or four-armed men guarding them, the slaves and George all seemed too nervous, surprised, and shocked to take a chance.

When the wagon pulled into Harpers Ferry, the quiet streets cast an eerie silence through the air. A slight drizzle was falling, which added a misty quality to the already strange night. It looked to George that only he and the other people in the wagon knew a raid was taking place. Maybe the raid wasn't as big as George had feared, or maybe it wasn't even a raid at all!

The wagon slowly approached its destination. George squinted in the darkness and saw armed guards, dressed in gray, surrounding the huge armory complex that was guarded by a long, brick wall with an iron-gated fence on top. As the wagon passed through the main gate, George noticed at least five or ten tall, brick buildings in the complex. Unfortunately, George had no time to study the layout of the place to figure out some possible escape route.

Immediately upon entering the grounds, the wagon stopped and the raiders jumped out onto the dirt courtyard. A bearded man, with fierce burning eyes, a large nose, and ears protruding outside of his graying hair and battered old cap, approached the wagon. Everyone's eyes followed him as he walked.

Memories flashed through George's mind: the fear and curiosity that he experienced in school when he had heard, for the first time, of John Brown and the massacre at Pottawatomie; the paper envelope of money with Brown's name printed on it, which David had stolen from his grandfather; the reaction of people in Kansas, like Charles, who feared and respected the very mention of Brown's name; his uncle's admiration and love for Brown, which led to his death; and now to George's imprisonment at the armory. All these images and emotions overpowered him as he remembered days, months, and even years of his life which had been affected in small ways by the action of this man. And finally, here was John Brown standing as powerful and scary as George had imagined him to be.

"Was this it?" George thought. "Had his whole life been designed to bring him to John Brown? Was it going to end here, in the middle of the night in some strange town with his uncle now dead and his father nowhere to be seen?"

"No! No!" George cried to himself as he struggled to control his fear. "This can't be it. My life means more than that and I won't let this man control me!"

Unaware of the struggle going on within George, Brown walked to the wagon and stared directly at the prisoners. His eyes contained so much fury that George had to turn his head to avoid eye contact with the man.

"Everything go alright, Aaron?" Brown asked. When he spoke, his deep voice was filled with emotion, and everyone, including the hostages, stopped and listened.

"No problems, sir," Aaron replied. "We went to Colonel Washington's house and found him right where you said. He came along quietly with his four slaves."

"Did you get the items?" Brown said anxiously.

"Right here, sir," Aaron said, handing a sword and a pistol to Brown. "The sword of George Washington himself."

Brown grabbed the items with a rush of excitement, looking at them as if they were holy symbols from God.

"Yes, yes!" he said, swinging the sword high in the air. "Now my destiny is complete. Just as our beloved George Washington once slew the British dragon for our freedom in the American Revolution, so too will I slay the dragons binding the Negroes in slavery!"

He held the sword up in the air as the raiders all cheered.

"And who is this?" Brown said, turning his head towards George. The sudden change in Brown's attitude and attention caught George by surprise.

"Some kid we picked up on the road," Aaron answered before George could say anything.

"Where are you from, boy?" Brown barked at George.

"Ah...ah Cumberland," George lied. He didn't dare tell Brown the truth.

Brown continued to stare at him in a disturbing silence.

"Cumberland, Maryland," George continued quickly. "My dad sent me to Harpers Ferry to—"

"Enough, boy," Brown interrupted, abruptly turning his attention away from George and to the freed slaves. "You slaves are free. By the authority vested in me by the Lord himself, I grant you your freedom and ask that you help us in freeing all of your kind who are so enslaved."

The slaves looked nervously at each other unsure of what to do or to say. Brown quickly took advantage of their indecisiveness to bark out orders.

"Aaron, hand them these pikes," he ordered. "And you freedmen, take the hostages into the building over there and guard them."

After the raiders handed the pikes to the freed slaves they watched them lead the hostages into the nearest building. George moved slowly from the wagon, trying to look around for a way of fleeing, until someone poked him in the back with a pike forcing him to move along more quickly.

Walking into the darkened building, George realized that there was no one to help him now. His father was lost somewhere on a lonely road, waiting for a stranger or for George to send help. The townspeople seemed unaware of the trouble they faced. Brown had captured a Federal arsenal loaded with guns and ammunition. Even if the Union army arrived, George knew Brown would sacrifice all the hostages before surrendering. His heart sank. It seemed hopeless.

The hostages in the engine room during the Harpers Ferry insurrection

Chapter 16
The Battle

George woke up in the engine room. It appeared to be one large room with a dusty floor and large doors and windows. It was obviously a place where they kept the local fire engines.

"Get in!" George heard a voice shout from outside as the door opened and the early morning sunlight momentarily lit the room.

A man was flung into the room from outside. Stumbling, he fell a few feet away from George. He didn't appear to be anyone special, probably another scared worker from the arsenal who Brown would add to the number of hostages slowly filling the room.

George realized that he must have only slept a short time. He felt exhausted and sick. His stomach was turning from hunger, and he felt a strong urge to go to the bathroom. Despite the heaviness in his head and the weakness in his body, he forced himself to stay awake and pay attention. Looking around, he figured there were approximately 40 hostages sitting on the floor or leaning against the wall, all crammed into the same room. Most of them were workers from the arsenal who had been caught by surprise when they showed up for work. The guards, mostly freedmen, paced nervously as the pikes shook in their hands. George thought they looked more like prisoners than willing followers of John Brown. Several raiders looked out the window. George wondered how many men consisted of Brown's "army." By overhearing talk he realized that some of Brown's men were scattered around the town cutting telegraph lines or guarding bridges.

A gunshot rang out from outside the engine house, followed by several more. Hearing shouts and movement, the hostages in the room moved towards the windows.

"Stay back!" a raider yelled as he pointed his gun at the hostages.

Quiet returned as the noises outside abruptly ceased, and the hostages returned nervously to their positions.

More shots and noises filled the air.

"They killed him, they killed him!" George could hear people shouting from outside.

It had begun, George realized. The townspeople must have found out what was happening and they were coming to stop Brown, but it sounded as if so far, Brown was stopping them.

Again the room became silent. Some men paced the floor while others looked nervously around the room. George sat in the corner holding his legs and thinking about his father. Would he ever find out what happened to him?

The door opened again allowing more sunlight to brighten the room. At first George could not tell who entered because the sudden change in light bathed the man's body in a shadow. When the door closed George recognized it to be John Brown. A chill rolled along George's spine.

"It has begun," Brown said simply.

"What has begun?" one of the hostages asked quickly.

"The battle to end slavery," Brown said simply. "As I expected, the citizens of this town have attempted to fight back and prevent us from completing our mission. They will not succeed. Soon, the masses of slaves will rise up to join our cause and you will see the dawning of a new age over this land."

"And what is to become of us," another hostage asked.

"You will be used as a human shield to protect my men," Brown said. "And once the battle is over, you will be released."

George didn't like the word "shield." Did Brown mean that they would actually hide behind the hostages when it came to that? George imagined bullets piercing his body as he shuddered.

"But what if these slaves never come to help you?" another hostage asked.

"They will," Brown answered simply as if he had no doubt in his mind.

"Sir," one of the raiders interrupted. "Several of the hostages have complained about food."

"Hmmm, yes," Brown replied, putting his hand to his chin and stroking his new beard. "I seem to have overlooked that."

George listed to his stomach growl from hunger. It had been more than 12 hours since he had eaten and he was beginning to feel dizzy. Most of the other hostages had eaten breakfast before their capture, but George had been held captive all night without food or drink.

"You there!" Brown said suddenly, pointing to a weak older man in the corner. "Stand up!"

The man got up slowly and stared at Brown.

"Y-yes," he stuttered nervously, unsure of what would be done to him.

"You are to be released," Brown said quickly. "And in exchange you will see to it that the hostages and my men are all fed breakfast. Do you understand?"

"I think so," the man replied.

George let out a deep sigh of relief as Brown went outside with the man. Finally, he would get something to eat!

The food took a while to arrive. It seemed like forever to George with his hunger being so great. Gulping down the food, he realized that he was the only one eating. George looked up at the others.

"Why aren't you eating?" George asked.

"We overheard the raiders talking," an 18-year-old boy replied. "They are afraid the food might be poisoned, so they aren't touching it."

"Poisoned!" George shouted, spitting out the food onto the floor and hacking up as much as he could. A few of the raiders looked suspiciously at George.

"Why would it be poisoned?" George cried.

"Since the food is for everyone here, including the raiders, Brown thinks that maybe the townspeople will poison the food to stop the raid," the boy answered.

"But then they'd kill us," George cried.

"Maybe," the boy said. "Or maybe make us real sick, or maybe we aren't that important but getting rid of these guys is. Who knows?"

"Shut up, you two," one of the guards said.

The boy shrugged his shoulders and turned away. George looked at his food. His stomach cried out for more and his parched throat begged for a drink, but George was too afraid. With a depressed shrug, he pushed the food away, leaned back against the wall, and closed his eyes.

Later, George was again awakened by noises.

"They got Newby, they got Newby!" a bearded man shouted as he burst into the room. He and another bearded man were breathing hard, carrying their rifles at their sides, and searching the room with their eyes. They headed towards Brown.

"Sir, sir," one of them reported. "Newby's been killed! We were guarding the bridge as you ordered when a company of armed militia attacked us. They completely overran us and we had to make our way here."

"Damn," Brown said simply as he began to pace.

"Sir!" the man went on. "What are we to do?"

Brown made no attempt to answer him.

"Sir!" the man repeated.

Brown continued to pace back and forth while everyone stared at him. He was mumbling something under his breath, which George could not understand. Was he confused and upset by these turn of events, or was this all a part of his plan? Brown seemed surprised and upset at the news, so George felt that this was not something Brown had expected. Maybe he would even give up! Or, maybe he would decide to use the hostages, George thought suddenly in a panic.

When Brown started looking over the hostages and moving towards George's direction, his heart raced, for he feared that Brown was going to single him out.

"You!" Brown shouted. "Get up!"

George's face whitened and his body quivered. Unexpectedly, the man next to him quickly stood up and took George's place.

"Yes?" the hostage said.

George leaned his head against the wall and breathed a sigh of relief.

"You are to be used to set up a truce," Brown said to the man.

"William," Brown continued, turning to the man who had reported Newby's death, "come over here."

"Yes," William said quickly.

"Take this hostage outside with a white flag of truce and see if you can get someone in authority to speak to me."

"Yes, sir," William answered quickly as he and the hostage headed towards the door. George felt a mixture of relief and disappointment as he realized that he could have been the one to be set free. Immediately, shouts and screams came from outside causing George to be thankful he had not been chosen.

"They've taken William!" a raider who was watching from a window shouted to Brown. "They're ignoring the truce and dragging him across the street."

"Lord!" Brown prayed as he looked skyward. "What must I do to please you?"

"Watson!" Brown yelled to his son who had been with him on the raid since the beginning. "You and Stevens take the superintendent and try again. Perhaps they will be more willing to talk if we release him."

"Yes, sir," they both answered walking across the room and ordering the superintendent to stand up and follow them outside.

Everyone in the room waited in silence anticipating what would happen next. George crossed his fingers hoping that a truce would be arranged so he would be set free.

Suddenly, gunshots and screams were heard and everyone in the room panicked.

"Silence!" Brown commanded as he turned to the hostages, motioning them back to their positions.

The door opened abruptly. "Father!" Watson cried as he dragged himself inside. "I am shot."

Everyone stared at Brown's son who had collapsed on the floor. Shots could be heard outside as bullets continued to ricochet around the courtyard. Brown slammed the door and looked down at his fallen son in silence.

"Excuse me, sir," one of the hostages suddenly said, breaking the silence. "Your other man is lying wounded in the yard."

"Yes, what of it?" Brown snapped.

"I volunteer to go out there and help him," the man replied simply. All eyes in the room stared in shock at this man. Was he crazy? He would be killed.

"What is to prevent you from simply running away?" Brown asked.

"I give you my word that once your man is safe I shall return."

Brown looked around the room considering the man's offer. He had more than enough hostages to spare, so even if this man did run off he would be in no worse situation. Besides, he couldn't stand and watch his loyal soldier die.

"Alright," Brown answered. "You may go."

Another raider quickly opened the door to let the hostage out. As he walked out the door, everyone rushed forward to watch or to listen.

George could barely see through the crowd, but because of his size he was able to squeeze in a look at the courtyard. The man walked bravely towards the wounded raider as bullets flew all around him. Reaching the spot where Stevens lay, the hostage bent down, picked him up, and dragged him across the street to the waiting townspeople. Incredibly, George watched as the man turned around and walked back to where he and the other hostages were waiting.

The door opened.

"Your man is receiving medical attention," the hostage reported as he sat down in his original place of imprisonment.

George turned to the man in shock and asked, "Why didn't you escape?"

"I gave my word," the man said simply.

The battle continued. George remained in his spot watching intensely, wondering what would happen. Shots were exchanged back and forth, one bullet bouncing off a brick and shattering the wall right next to George's ear. Quickly, George put his head down and covered his ears with his hands. He ignored the hungry growl in his gut and just waited.

By now, Brown's men had killed several townspeople including the mayor. In reaction, the hostile crowd surrounding the arsenal began to fire more shots into the room. The firing became almost constant now, and at one point, John Brown's other son, Oliver, was mortally wounded.

Hours and hours passed with no changes. The townspeople continued to fire into the house. At one point, a group of men charged at the house and had almost rescued the hostages. Brown's men managed to force them back.

The passing of day into night only depressed George even more. He had grown so hungry that he could not think straight, and the groaning of Brown's men dying on the floor only added to George's panic. Brown himself seemed to be losing it when at one point he yelled at his dying son.

"If you must die, then die like a man!"

"What kind of a man is this John Brown?" George thought to himself, "who is willing to watch his own sons die on the floor. My God, if he treats them that way, what will become of us?"

U.S. Marines storming the engine house

Chapter 17
The Marines

Colonel Robert E. Lee studied the situation. It was early in the morning of the next day and Lee had rushed so quickly to Harpers Ferry from Washington, D.C., that he did not even have time to put on his uniform.

"Colonel Shriver," Lee began. "While I am in command of the Marines under the authority of President Buchanan, I believe this to be a state matter. As commander of the Maryland Volunteers, would you like the honor of assaulting first?"[1]

Colonel Shriver looked around. The dark morning air was alive with activity. Although the fighting had for the most part stopped due to the fear of hurting the hostages, the movement of townspeople and troops had not. Over 90 U.S. Marines had arrived during the night to join his force as well as several other militias. Townspeople were gathered around the arsenal, shooting off their guns or their mouths, or sitting and getting drunk in the nearby saloons. A surrender order,

---

1. This conversation is based on one that actually happened on the night of October 17, 1859, between Lee and the men described. Text of the discussion is taken from the Harpers Ferry National Park Guidebook entitled *John Brown's Raid.*

which Lee had written to Brown several hours ago, had already been rejected, and it looked as if the engine house would have to be stormed.

"No thank you, sir," Colonel Shriver finally said. "These men of mine have wives and children. I will not expose them to such risks. You are paid for doing this kind of work."

Lee then offered Colonel Baylor of the Virginia militia the same opportunity, but he also turned it down for the same reason.

"Lieutenant Green," Lee said finally, turning to the man in direct charge of the marines. "Would you like the honor of taking these men out?"

"Thank you, sir," Green said, lifting his cap. "I would be honored."

Lee then instructed Green to choose a small storming party and be prepared to assault at first light. Lee did not want to hurt any of the hostages, so he instructed his men to use only their bayonets and not to fire.

Around seven in the morning, Lieutenant J.E.B. Stuart who had accompanied Lee from Washington, D.C., was sent to bring the surrender note to Brown. Approaching the engine house, Stuart knocked lightly on the door. It opened slowly.

Staring Stuart in the face was John Brown himself, his body propped against the door to prevent any looks inside, and a cocked rifle in one hand. Stuart read the surrender terms to Brown.

Lee demanded Brown's total surrender. While he would try to spare as many lives as possible, Lee could not guarantee that Brown would survive if he did not surrender immediately. Upon hearing this, Brown responded with demands of his own—to be allowed to cross the river with the hostages safely; otherwise, no deal was to be made.

Stuart backed away from Brown as he waved his hat.

"The signal!" Colonel Lee thought as he looked over at the 12 marines waiting to charge.

The door slammed shut. George had been watching and listening intently to the conversation, hoping that somehow Brown would agree to release him. Now, the situation looked as if it would get really ugly. George and the others would, indeed, be used as a human shield. He prayed to God to spare him.

"Prepare yourselves," Brown shouted to the remaining raiders. "I believe an attack is imminent!"

George heard pounding on the door and watched as Brown's men stood back and waited. The pounding stopped abruptly; however, noises and shouts could be heard outside. Again, a pounding on the door, this time much louder.

"They're gonna come through!" George thought in excitement.

A second loud strike on the door opened up a small hole forcing a ladder through the door. Then, it was pulled back out enabling a soldier in uniform to crawl through it.

"Fire!" Brown commanded as two more soldiers tried to enter into the room.

George watched as the next two soldiers dropped dead on the floor. One of them had been shot in the groin while the other man had his face pierced by a bullet. Blood splattered everywhere. George and the other hostages quickly moved to the back of the room to hide.

More marines entered the building unharmed to seize Brown's men. One of the hostages, the man whom Brown had stolen the gun and sword from earlier, rushed forward to point out John Brown to the commander. Brown turned just in time to feel the edge of Lieutenant Green's sword smash into the back of his neck. Brown fell.

Within three minutes, two of Brown's men were already dead while the remaining two surrendered. The slaves never put up a fight. Brown who had been beaten senseless by Lieutenant Green was still alive. The fight was over.

It all had happened so fast that George and the others couldn't believe the siege was over. He looked around the room at the other hostages who were just as shocked as he was. Suddenly, George let out a cheer and everyone joined in. They were free!

The soldiers cleared out the raiders and checked on the hostages. In the confusion, no one noticed George sneak out to stare at the man who had almost started a revolution and nearly ended George's life.

Brown lay there, silently, blood slowly flowing out of his wounds. Amazingly, he didn't look that threatening anymore. He just looked old and tired. It was hard to believe that this one man could cause so much trouble and scare so many people.

The crowd moved in closer to get a look at the person who had threatened their town and sent panic through every man, woman, and child. The slave revolt in southern Virginia 27 years ago, which had seen whites overrun and killed by angry blacks, was still fresh on the minds of the townspeople. Brown's raid reminded them of how dangerous a slave rebellion was and of how violent the slaves could become if threatened.

George dropped back to prevent himself from being crushed by the crowd. Suddenly, he heard a familiar voice.

"George! George!"

"Dad?" George wondered in amazement. "Dad, is that you?"

"Over here!" his father called. "I'm in the back!"

George strained his neck to look over the crowd to find his father standing alone, waving at him and leaning on a crutch.

"Dad!" George shouted in sheer joy and relief. "Dad, you're here!"

Running over to his father, George hugged him so tight he almost knocked him down.

"How did you get here?" George asked in his excitement. "How did you know I was here? What happened to your leg? Are you alright?"

"Slow down, slow down," his father said laughing. "I'll explain everything."

As the two backed away from the crowd, George's father explained that he had only spent the one night on the road before a friendly traveler helped him into town. His leg was fine, probably some kind of fracture that would heal soon enough. What he really wanted to know was what had happened to George.

"Oh, Dad, it was horrible," George began. "Absolutely horrible. I went straight down the road just like you said, but I musta got lost somehow and took a wrong turn somewhere. It was dark and rainy and I didn't know what to do. Then, this man stopped me, pointed a gun at me, and told me to get in a wagon. He was one of Brown's men and they had taken me prisoner!"

"My Lord," George's dad exclaimed, sitting back and shaking his head. "I never should have let you go off alone."

"Don't worry about it, Dad," George said softly, putting his hand on his father's shoulder. "You had to do it. You had no idea what Brown was up to and everything turned out alright anyway."

"But you could have been killed!"

"But I wasn't," George said simply.

George's father looked at him and smiled.

"C'mere," he laughed, grabbing George's head and rubbing his hair until George thought it would fall out. George laughed as the two of them hugged again.

"You hungry?" his father said finally.

"My God," George answered quickly. "You don't know the half of it!"

As father and son stood up and headed out of the arsenal, George looked back one final time to see the crowd dispersing. The raid had failed.

Chapter 18
The Hanging

George sat back in the chair. After finishing another letter to David, it did not make him feel any better. A month had passed since the raid ended, and George continued to feel guilty about what had happened to his Uncle John.

George and his father were supposed to have saved him. They were supposed to have ridden boldly off to find David's father and return him safely to Lawrence while David stayed home alone to look after his sick mother. Instead, George had to tell David that not only was his father not coming back ever again but that George and his dad had almost been the ones who had killed him.

At least he didn't have to face David, George thought. With Sean still waiting for his leg to heal, they were in no position to go anywhere, so they had remained in Harpers Ferry. George was very glad about this because it also meant that he could see what would finally happen with John Brown.

Even though John Brown had survived the raid, he had been wounded so badly that he could barely stand. The government would not let that stop their prosecution of him. They forced Brown to lie on a cot during his trial. People from all over the country had rushed to nearby Charles Town to watch the trial. Reporters, lawyers, slave owners, abolitionists, and even salesmen had come to find out what would be done with old Brown or to take advantage of the trial to make a quick buck off all the other people there. George and his father had been lucky that they had been there from the beginning, or they never would have found a room! The strange thing was, George noticed, that the trial had seemed to turn into a debate on slavery. At one point it seemed as though the South was on trial for holding slaves instead of John Brown trying to set them free!

The local militias had stayed around the area, for people were nervous that somehow the slaves might rebel or that some of the abolitionists, who had promised to set Brown free, would actually carry out their threats. This town was actually busier and crazier than Boston had ever been, George thought.

Although the trial was over in less than a week, the area didn't get any quieter. Brown had been found guilty and sentenced to die, but the crowds of people outside of the courtroom did not find enough satisfaction with the verdict. They wanted to see the execution. They wanted to see the man, whom they feared so much, pay for his crimes and they wanted this symbol of taking up weapons against slavery finally snuffed out of existence. George wanted to see the execution too.

Every day, George went to Charles Town to watch the trial. When it was over, he still wandered to town to listen to the crowds and to watch all the activity. George was amazed so many people felt so differently about this man.

"I don't understand it, Dad," George said to his father one day back at the hotel. "How can some people say that Brown is actually innocent?"

"You lived in Kansas for a while, son," his father began while sitting on his bed, washing and rubbing his sore leg in an attempt to get rid of the aches and pains.

"I know," George answered. "But that was different. People were fighting over different opinions or fighting to get land back or for revenge. How can people fight over this? Everyone knows he did it. Brown admitted to it."

"Life is never that easy, son," Sean answered. "Even though you saw Brown commit his crimes with your own eyes, other people say that the reason he did it makes him innocent."

"Do you think that killing people to free the slaves is O.K.?" George exclaimed.

"No, of course not, son," his father answered quickly. "But at the same time you have to admire someone who is willing to fight and die for what he believes."

"No, I don't have to admire him!" George replied sharply. "The man is a monster! He kept me prisoner, starved me, and yelled and screamed like some crazy man the whole time."

"That's not what you said before," his father said slowly. He could see that George was very upset about the whole thing and that he had probably even had nightmares afterwards.

"That was before everyone started defending him," George answered. "I mean, I was there, Dad. I watched as he kidnaped people and held them hostage. I listened to him talk about his holy war, saying he got power from God and all that stuff. I even watched as he stood over his two dying sons ignoring their pain because he wanted to win."

The room was silent for a minute. George took a deep breath. He hadn't realized how much this bothered him.

"You would never leave me to fight for some cause would you, Dad?" George asked slowly.

"What do you mean, son?"

"Well," George began. "When I watched how Brown ignored his son's feelings and went on with his fight, I was wondering what would happen if you ever had to go fight in some war or something else. Kinda like what David's dad did."

"I'm not a soldier or an abolitionist," his dad said simply, trying to avoid the question.

"No, I know that, Dad," George said a little annoyed. "But if you really strongly believed in something and you had to leave me or sacrifice me to help your cause, would you do it?"

"Wow," George's dad said with a deep breath of air. "I certainly hope not."

"You hope not?" George repeated.

"Well, yes," he answered. "After all, no man knows what the future will bring. Don't get me wrong, son. I love you with all my heart and would fight with my last breath to defend you, but what if we were at war or something and if I didn't go our country would lose the war. You'd die anyway."

"I guess so," George answered.

"Besides," his dad went on, this time with a little more confidence. "Sometimes being a man comes with certain responsibilities. You can't always do what you want even if it means your life or your family's. You got to remember your duty to God and your country as well."

"I guess so," George repeated softly. He understood what his dad was saying but that didn't mean he liked it any more.

Suddenly, a knock on the door shattered the silence.

"Who is it?" George's dad called out.

"It's David," said the voice from the other side of the door.

"David?" George gasped as he and his father stared open-mouthed at each other. "How did he get here?"

"Don't just stand there, son, let him in."

George walked over to the door, shaking his head in disbelief.

"My God," George mumbled to himself as his hand reached for the door. "What will I say to him?"

"Hi, George," David said with very little emotion as the door opened in front of him. "How are you?"

"Oh...O.K., I guess," George answered. He had never felt so uncomfortable in his life. There was no joy in seeing David. There was no hugging or even shaking hands. There was only awkward silence.

"Let him in, George," his father called from the back.

George stepped away from the door for David to enter.

"Hi, Uncle Sean," David said with as little emotion as before.

"David, my Lord, David," his uncle began. "How did you get here? Where is your mother?"

"She's dead," David said blankly, without offering any other explanation. He simply stood there coldly, expressionless, like a robot waiting for a reason to talk.

"Dead?" his Uncle Sean and George repeated. "What happened?"

"She never recovered," David began. He was still standing in the middle of the room not making any attempt to be comfortable. "She kept getting sicker and sicker. When the letter came saying that my father was dead, she simply lost all her strength and died in a day or two."

"Oh, Lord," Uncle Sean cried, putting his head down into his hands. Tears were beginning to build up inside of him. Regina had been much more to him than just a sister-in-law. She had been a beautiful, trusted friend to both him and George. In fact, ever since Sean's wife died, Regina had been almost like a mother to George.

George too was frozen in shock. Now both of David's parents were dead, and George could not help feeling responsible. What had they done? What could they do now?

"After she died, I gathered up all my things and made my way here," David continued, ignoring their grief. "I needed to see your faces one last time."

Uncle Sean lifted his face from his hands.

"What do you mean, one last time?" he asked.

"I'm leaving," David answered. "I'm leaving you, Kansas, the family—this whole mess."

"But why?" George asked.

"Isn't that obvious?" David answered sharply. "I've got nowhere to go and nothing to do. I'm all alone now."

"You've got us," George said softly.

"You?" David yelled. "You? How could I stay with you? You're the ones who killed them! You killed my dad and mom just as surely as if you shot them."

"Now just a minute, David," Uncle Sean interrupted.

"You didn't actually pull the trigger, but you might as well have," David went on.

"You're crazy, David!" George said, walking to where David stood. "I told you in the letter that we were trying to stop him when he fell backwards over a cliff!"

"You always hated him," David continued, ignoring George's comment completely. "You thought he was stupid and strange and that he was a terrible father."

George had no answer to that statement. In a way, David was right and the silence made David all the angrier.

"Well, he was a great man," David went on. "A better man than any of you!"

George backed away again from David, who was starting to get really crazy.

"He believed in something important," David shouted through tears. "And he died for it. While you two sit there and make fun of him I'm standing here without a father because he had the guts to fight and die for what he believed in!"

"I respected his beliefs," George's dad said. "And I might have even agreed with him in some areas, but you know I couldn't agree with his methods."

"What he was doing was right!" David yelled.

"It's never right to kill someone!" George yelled back. He wasn't about to let David blame this whole mess on them.

"It is if it's for a greater cause!" David shouted.

"You're as nuts as your old man!" George yelled back. As soon as he said those words he wished he hadn't.

"Don't you call me nuts!" David yelled as he ran at George knocking him onto the floor.

The two of them rolled around for a few seconds trying to punch each other without either of them landing a blow.

"Stop it, you two!" Sean yelled. "Stop it right now!"

The boys ignored him and continued to fight. David who was not only bigger and stronger than George was also much, much angrier. Using all his strength he rolled George onto the floor and sat upon his stomach. Before George could squirm away, David punched him solidly in the face.

"Aaahh," George cried as blood from his nose and chin splattered onto David's shirt. But David didn't stop. He hit George all the harder making his face move to and fro with each punch.

"That's enough!" Sean yelled as he grabbed David by the back of the neck throwing him against the far wall. It had taken Sean several seconds to get up on his bad leg, and the strength which he needed to throw David caused spasms of pain to shoot up his leg again.

"Aaaahh, damn," Sean cried as he grabbed his leg and looked at David. "Why did you have to go and do that, David?"

David said nothing as he wiped the blood off his face and stared at his uncle.

"Are you alright, George?" his father said as he slowly leaned down to look over his son. Blood covered George's face, and his cheeks were beginning to swell.

"I...I think so," George mumbled.

"Listen, David," his Uncle Sean spoke angrily as he spun around to face his nephew. "I understand how you must feel about losing your folks, but frankly I don't know why you think we killed your father, or how you can blame us for this mess we're all in. All I know is I'm not gonna let you accuse George or make us feel that we did something wrong. Heck, if it weren't for you and your father running off to Kansas in the first place, none of this would have ever happened."

"You don't have to worry about me bothering you anymore, Uncle Sean," David said harshly as he spit on the floor. "I've seen all I need to see of you. You're just as bad as everyone else who pretends that there isn't any problem."

George and his father stared at David not exactly sure what he was getting at.

"I'm outta here anyways," David said as he turned to walk out the door. "See ya around."

George and his father simply stared out the door in disbelief as David disappeared.

"C'mon, son, let's get you cleaned up," George's dad said helping his son to his feet.

For several weeks George and his father continued to heal their many wounds. David had disappeared from sight, and even though George still felt bad about what had happened, he didn't miss him. They had been best friends as well as cousins, but lately, David had grown really strange, as he became more concerned with all kinds of talk and abolitionist stuff instead of just hanging out. George knew that both of them had been through a lot these past couple of years and they had changed. What George didn't know was whether he would ever see his cousin again.

The day of Brown's hanging finally came. People from all over the country had continued to remain interested in John Brown who had become such an important issue that stories, poems, and letters were written about this man who had dared to take up arms against the government. Some people saw him as a hero, others saw him as a demon, and most primarily saw him as a confused or possibly insane man.

The crowd gathered as early as dawn around the courthouse. No one except the soldiers were allowed near the execution area, so people had to be content with seeing Brown march out of the courthouse and be taken by wagon to the execution field. By the time the old man stepped slowly out into the light the crowd had become quite large.

"Killer!" someone yelled.

"God be with you!" yelled another.

Shouts and accusations flew at the man. The soldiers had cleared a path from the courthouse to the wagon and no one was allowed to cross it. The people had lined up along the path on both sides pushing and shoving to get a look at Brown. George's size allowed him to squeeze up to the front directly opposite the people on the other side of the line.

As Brown walked from the courthouse down the path, everyone grew silent and watched. He was unbelievably calm and quiet. His eyes stared straight ahead. Clearly, he was thinking or praying. Stopping for a minute, he looked at the crowd which made no move or sound as his piercing eyes looked among them for something or someone. George tried to look in the same direction where Brown was staring, but there didn't seem to be any one person or thing that Brown was looking at. Then George saw him.

David, standing directly across the path from George, was looking up at the old man.

"David's still in town!" George thought to himself as he tried to get his cousin's attention.

David was too busy looking at John Brown to notice George. It was almost as though Brown held some kind of spell over David whose eyes appeared blank and his feet shifted back and forth. What was it about John Brown that fascinated David so much?

"Who are you?" David thought out loud as he continued to stare. "Why did my father follow you so faithfully and why are you so content to join him in heaven?"

Brown gave no answer.

"Are you looking at me?" David continued to himself. "Do you see something in me that reminds you of my dad? I hope so."

"Wait, don't go!" David cried as Brown continued to walk down the path towards the wagon. "I have so much I want to ask you. What should I do now? How can I help? Where should I go?"

David wondered more and more what he should do. His parents were gone, but their mission was not yet completed. Slavery still existed and until it was abolished, his parents would never rest in peace. David's memories raced back and forth recalling all the things that his parents had done as abolitionists in Kansas and in Boston. Suddenly, he remembered his friend Lisa who had escaped to Boston only to be captured and sent back to the South.

David smiled. It was a sneaky, awkward smile as if he were planning something. When he turned, George stood directly across from him. He smiled once more at his cousin and turned away.

"Wait, David, wait!" George called, but it was too late. David was gone, and George wondered what that smile meant on David's face.

The crowd cheered. Brown was sitting in the wagon on top of the coffin waiting to be taken away for his execution. The nightmare would soon be over.

Epilogue
John Brown's Body

It wasn't over. The nightmare was only beginning. John Brown's spirit continued to haunt the country after his hanging. Northern abolitionists saw Brown as a hero. Southerners saw this as proof that they could not live with the Northerners. Although John Brown had failed to free the slaves in Virginia, he had succeeded in stretching the bonds between North and South to the breaking point. To some people, it was not a matter of whether North and South would separate, but when.

It was also a turning point for George and David. After seeing Brown praised in the North, George and his father were so disgusted with this attitude that they decided to never return to Boston. While staying at Harpers Ferry, they met some men from the Richmond Gray's militia who had come for the execution. One of them, a man named John Wilkes Booth, suggested they move to Richmond, a lovely city where they would have no problem finding a job.

David had disappeared completely. His brothers and sisters stayed to live with their Uncle Robert, who had decided to leave Boston as well to move to Pennsylvania. Grampa William had kicked them out of the house once his daughter, Regina, had died.

George thought it was almost funny that they had been split like the country. Where North and South were finding they could no longer live together, the same thing was happening to George's family. It was not that they didn't love each other; quite the opposite. George would forever miss the family dinners, the stories of Aunt Patricia, and the wrestling matches between David and Josh. The family had too many problems that could not get resolved. Maybe, they could still be friends. Maybe, this separation was only temporary, George hoped. Unfortunately, if they ever did see each other again, George knew it would never be the same.

Author's Note

The title of this book, *On the Trail of John Brown's Body*, was somewhat misleading. As you now know, when George finally found John Brown, he was very much alive. This title was chosen, however, because of the lingering effect John Brown's body would have on the country after his death.

Brown became a symbol for the abolition of slavery. After he died, North and South continued to debate, threaten, and try to outdo each other regarding the subject of slavery. By the time Abraham Lincoln was elected, many people in the South had had enough discussion, so they decided to separate from the Union. This, of course, resulted in the beginning of the Civil War. The importance of John Brown to the feelings of the war is documented in a song that some Union soldiers sang as they marched off to bring the Southerners back into the Union. Two verses and the chorus went something like this:

> *John Brown's body lies a-mouldering in the grave,*
> *John Brown's body lies a-mouldering in the grave,*
> *John Brown's body lies a-mouldering in the grave,*
> *But his soul goes marching on.*

Chorus:

Glory, Glory, Hallelujah
Glory, Glory, Hallelujah
Glory, Glory, Hallelujah
His soul goes marching on.

He's gone to be a soldier in the Army of the Lord
He's gone to be a soldier in the Army of the Lord
He's gone to be a soldier in the Army of the Lord
His soul goes marching on.[1]

John Brown's body haunted the nation. For some abolitionists, it was a symbol of the holiness of their cause. For some Southerners, it was a symbol of the evil tyranny that the North wanted to impose on them. In the end, all that would matter was John Brown's terrible warning stated before he died:

> *I John Brown am now quite certain that the crimes of this guilty land will never be purged away; but with blood.*[2]

---

1. "John Brown's Body," Public Broadcasting Service Online.
2. This information is included on the *John Brown's Raid* videocassette produced by the Harpers Ferry Center. It is also discussed in Kenneth C. Davis's *Don't Know Much About the Civil War.* To learn more about John Brown and Harpers Ferry, Virginia, consult the bibliography.

Preview

Look for this scene in book three of the Young Heroes of History Series: *Off to Fight*

G eorge reached down, made another snowball, and placed it next to Eric.

"Great," Eric said gleefully, "we're just like the artillery boys. You supply the ammo and I'll do the firing. Keep up the good work. They seem to be falling back."

The snowball fight was becoming larger as news of it spread throughout the Army of Northern Virginia. Boys from the Virginia regiments had come in to reinforce George's unit. Other soldiers from Texas and Georgia had joined the opposition.

"It's becoming everyone against Virginia!" George cried.

"I'm gonna try to make it across the field to Bobby," Eric said suddenly. "You cover me."

"But," George argued as Eric darted out from the bush cover. Instantly, a mass of snowballs descended on Eric when he fell backwards a few steps.

"Cover me!" he yelled back to George.

"I am," George said laughing, "I am."

George hurled as many of the snowballs as he could at the other boys. Three or four balls hit and stopped the boys for a second, but it made no difference. Eric was bombarded from all sides by snowballs. They hit him in the legs, in the stomach, in the head, and on the butt. George couldn't help but laugh.

"Stop, stop!" Eric cried out, waving his hands as he stood.

Ten, twenty, thirty snowballs all fell upon Eric as he collapsed in a heap. A cheer sounded from the other side while Eric lay on his back in the snow.

"We ain't giving up yet!" George heard Bobby yell. "Fire!"

Snowballs from George's side of the field blasted the enemy. The boys staggered and started to fall back but not before three of them had grabbed Eric by the feet and dragged him towards their barricade.

"We gut ourselves a prisoner," they said laughing.

"George, help!" Eric screamed as he arched his neck while being dragged and looking back towards George. "Don't let these awful boys take me. Save me! Save meeeee!"

George laughed at Eric's antics.

"I suppose I should help him," George thought to himself. "Besides it will be fun sneaking behind enemy lines."

George walked slowly at first with his head lowered so the enemy could not see or hear his movements as he turned deeper into the woods. The best way for him to help Eric would be to swing out a little into the woods and then surprise the South Carolinians from behind. Realizing that the snow was hiding a lot of the noise of his movement, George increased his pace. "If only his feet weren't so cold," he thought.

George heard a noise ahead. He stopped suddenly. Was another soldier out here too?

Crack, a twig snapped and a figure moved.

"Gotcha!" George yelled as he hit the figure in the head with a snowball.

Whoever it was must have been surprised because they fell down almost immediately. George rushed forward.

"Uhhh, ah-uh, ah-uh."

George stopped and listened.

"The person was crying! What kind of timid soldier was this?" George thought.

"Hey, don't cry," George said in an annoyed tone as he approached the figure. "It was only a snowball."

George knelt beside him. He was too small to be a soldier. "Perhaps a drummer boy," George thought.

"I said don't cry," George repeated out loud as he turned the person over from its crouched position.

"Huh?" George exclaimed falling backwards in surprise as he stared open-mouthed at the small girl, who was slowly backing away from him. She was clothed in what looked to be a dress, but it was so torn and tattered that her skin shown through it, and her body vibrated noticeably in the cold.

"You're a girl?" George said slowly.

She said nothing. George knew by the look of terror on her face and in her deep blue eyes that this was no ordinary girl.

Bibliography

The All True Adventures of Lidie Newton. Lawrence Journal World. Journal World Archives Document Delivery. Http://newslibrary.krmediastream.c...nt/ jw_auth?DBLIST=jw97&DOCNUM=7517 8; August 2, 1999.

Allen, G. Freeman. *Railways.* New York, N.Y.: William, Morrow and Co., Inc., 1982.

Boyer, Paul S., and Clark E. Clifford, Jr., et al. *The Enduring Vision: A History of the American People.* Lexington, Ma.: D.C. Heath, 1990.

Crumrin, Timothy. *The Making of the National Road.* Http://www.connerprairie.org/cp/ntlroad.html; 1994.

Davis, Kenneth C. *Don't Know Much About the Civil War: Everything You Need to Know About America's Greatest Conflict but Never Learned.* New York, N.Y.: William Morrow and Co., Inc., 1996.

Early Politicians Left Mark on State. Lawrence Journal World. Journal World Archives Document Delivery. Http://newslibrary.krmediastream.c...nt/ jw_auth?DBLIST=jw97&DOCNUM=15503 8; August 2, 1999.

Fish, Carl Russell. *The Rise of the Common Man*. New York, N.Y.: The Macmillan Company, 1927.

Gilbert, David T. *Harpers Ferry National Park*. Http:// pigpen.itd.nps.gov/hafe/hf_info.htm; August 2, 1999.

Goodrich, Thomas. *War to the Knife*. Stackpole Books, 1998.

Handlin, Oscar. *Boston's Immigrants*. Atheneum, New York, 1972.

Hart, Albert Bushnell. *American History told by Contemporaries, Volume IV*. New York: The Macmillan Company, 1964.

Hickok, Ralph. *Baseball History*. Http://www. hickoksports.com/history/baseba02.shtml; 1999.

History of Adair Cabin/John Brown Museum. Http:// www.kshs.org/places/adarhist.htm; August 2, 1999.

How Lawrence Got its Name. Lawrence Journal World. Journal World Archives Document Delivery. Http:// n e w s l i b r a r y . k r m e d i a s t r e a m . c . . . n t / jw_auth?DBLIST=jw97&DOCNUM=2722 8; August 2, 1999.

Jansen, Steven. *Questions Re: Early Lawrence, e-mail to Alan Kay*. Lawrence, Kans.: Watkins Museum, August 25, 1999.

"John Brown's Body." Public Broadcasting Service Online. Visit Http://www.pbs.org/wgbh/amex/ brown/sfeature/song.html; August 2, 1999.

John Brown's Raid. Produced by Harpers Ferry Center. National Park Service. Harpers Ferry, Va.: Harpers Ferry Historical Association, 1985. Videocassette.

John Brown's Raid. National Park Service. Washington D.C.: Library of Congress, 1973.

Kent, Deborah. *Boston*. New York: Children's Press, 1998.

Kent, Zachary. *John Brown's Raid on Harpers Ferry*. Chicago, Ill.: Children's Press, 1988.

Lawrence Convention and Visitors Bureau Online. *Visit Lawrence.* Http://www.visitlawrence.com/history/civilwar.html; August 2, 1999.

McCutcheon, Marc. *Everyday Life in the 1800s.* Cincinnati, Ohio: Writer's Digest Books, 1993.

McPherson, James M. *Battle Cry of Freedom.* New York: Oxford University Press, 1988.

Monaghan, Jay. *Civil War on the Western Border.* New York: Bonanza Books, 1955.

Nevins, Allan. *The Needless Conflict: A Treasury of American Heritage.* New York: Simon & Schuster, 1960, 216–23.

Oates, Stephen B. *God's Angry Man, American History, Volume I, Article 27.* Guilford, Conn.: The Dushkin Publishing Group Inc., 1987.

Rae, Noel. *Witnessing America.* New York: Stonesong Press, 1996.

Smiley, Jane. *The All True Travels and Adventures of Lidie Newton.* New York: Alfred A. Knopf, 1998.

Stampp, Kenneth M. *The Peculiar Institution.* New York: Vintage Books, 1956.

Sutherland, James. *Lawrence City Directory.* Indianapolis, Ind.: James Sutherland, 1861.

Whitehill, Walter Muir. *Boston: A Topographical History.* Cambridge, Mass.: The Belknap Press of Harvard University, 1963.

Winckler, Suzanne. *The Smithsonian Guide to Historic America: The Plains States.* New York: Stewart, Tabori & Chang, 1990.

Woellhof, Brad. Telephone conversation with author. August 1999.

Years Past in Lawrence. Lawrence Public Library. Http://www.ci.lawrence.ks.us/yearspast/mass_st/mass_st.html; 1996.